F Adolphus

Some Memories of Paris

F Adolphus

Some Memories of Paris

ISBN/EAN: 9783743311404

Manufactured in Europe, USA, Canada, Australia, Japa

Cover: Foto ©Andreas Hilbeck / pixelio.de

Manufactured and distributed by brebook publishing software (www.brebook.com)

F Adolphus

Some Memories of Paris

SOME MEMORIES

OF

PARIS

BY

F. ADOLPHUS

NEW YORK

HENRY HOLT AND COMPANY

1895

CONTENTS.

SOME MEMORIES OF PARIS.

CHAPTER I.

THE STREETS FORTY YEARS AGO.

THE changes which have come about during the last forty years in the aspect of the streets of Paris have been vastly more marked than those which have occurred in London within the same period. The two main reasons of the difference are: firstly, that London set to work to modify its ways at a much earlier date than Paris, and that Paris still retained, at the commencement of the fifties, many remainders of ancient sights and customs, and still presented many characteristics of past days, which, on this side of the Channel, had faded out long before; secondly, that, when transformation did at last begin in Paris, it was far more sudden and violent, far more universal and radical, than the mild gradual variations we have introduced in London, and that, in consequence of the utterness of that transformation, an entire city was virtually swept away and a new one put in its place. The Paris of the First Empire was still visible in 1850, almost unaltered in its essential features ; old houses, old roadways, old vehicles, old cheapnesses, old particularities of all sorts, had been faithfully preserved, and struck both the eye and the pocket of the new-comer as signs of another epoch. It was not till Haussmann began, in 1854, the reconstruction, not only of so many of the buildings of Paris, but—what was far more grave — of its conditions, and practices, and order of existence, that the relics of former life, former manners, and former economies found themselves successively crushed out, and that the brilliant extravagant Paris of Napoleon III. was evolved from the ruins.

At the commencement of the Second Empire Paris was still a city of many mean streets and a few grand ones ; still a city of rare pavements, rough stones, stagnant gutters, and scarcely any drainage ; still a city of uncomfortable homes, of varied smells, of relatively simple life, and of close intermixture of classes.   This last element

—the intermixture of classes—exercised particular influence on the look of the streets as well
as on the home contacts of the inhabitants, and
needs to be borne always in mind in endeavour-
ing to reconstitute the former aspects of the
place. Of course there were, in those days as
always, certain quarters of the town which were
tenanted exclusively by the poor; but the great
feature was that the poor were not restricted to
those special quarters ; they lodged everywhere
else as well, wherever they found themselves in
proximity to their work, in the most aristocratic
as in the lowest districts. In almost every
house in the fashionable parts of Paris the suc-
cessive floors were inhabited by a regular grada-
tion of classes from the bottom to the top ; over
the rich people on the first and second floors
were clerks and tradespeople *en chambre* on the
third and fourth, and workmen of all sorts on
the fifth and sixth. Thorough mingling of
ranks under the same roof was the rule of life :
all the lodgers used the same stairs (in those
days back staircases scarcely existed); all
tramped up and down amidst the careless
spillings and droppings of the less clean portion
of the inmates. The most finished of the
women of the period thought it natural to use

the same flight as the dirty children from above them; a lady going out to dinner in white silk did not feel shocked at meeting a mason in white calico coming in; nodding acquaintances between fellow-lodgers were formed when time had taught them each other's faces. The effect of this amalgamation in the houses stretched out naturally into the streets, where, in consequence of the nearness of their homes, the various strata of the population of each quarter were thrown together far more promiscuously than they are now. The workers have no place in the new houses, which are built for the rich alone; they have been driven to the outskirts, instead of being spread, more or less, over the whole town: the classes and the masses live now entirely apart, in districts remote from each other, and the growing hate of the masses for the classes has been considerably stimulated by the separation. A totally altered social relationship, a far less friendly attitude and feeling between the top and the bottom, has resulted from the expulsion of so many of the poor from their old homes.

The good streets of Paris forty years ago were therefore far more generally representative than they are to-day. They exhibited the various components of the community with more abundance, more accuracy, and a truer average; universal blending was their normal condition.   The stranger learnt more from them in a day about types and categories than he can now learn in a week, for in the present state of things there are, in one direction, regions where a cloth coat is never beheld, and, in another, districts where a blouse is almost unknown.   And when to this former medley of persons and castes we add the notable differences of dress, of bearing, of occupations of the passers-by from those which prevail in the rich quarters now, the contrast of general effect may easily be imagined.   Forty years are but an instant in the history of a nation, and yet the last forty years have sufficed to produce an organic change in the appearance of the streets of Paris.

The change extends to everything—to the houses, the shops, the public and private carriages, the soldiers, the policemen, the hawkers' barrows, and the aspect of the men and women. Nearly everything has grown smarter, but everything without exception has grown dearer. Whether the former compensates for the latter is a question which every one must decide for himself according to his personal view.

The shops were of course inferior to what they are now. The show in the windows—the *montre*, as the French call it—was less brilliant and less tempting. They were, however, the prettiest of their time in Europe; and all that they have done since has been to march onward with the century, and, amidst the general progress of the world, to keep the front place they held before. Stores, in the English sense, have never become acclimatised in Paris (though several attempts have been made to introduce them), mainly because the cooks refuse to purchase food in places where they can get no commission for themselves; but the growth of the Bon Marché and the Louvre, which has been entirely effected within the last forty years, supplies evidence enough that in Paris, as in London, the tendency of the period—outside the cooks—is towards comprehensive establishments, where objects of many natures can be found at low prices under the same roof. Potin, the universal grocer, supplies even an example of success in spite of the cooks. Yet, notwithstanding the competition of the new menageries of goods, most of the shop windows on the Boulevards and in the Rue de la Paix seem to indicate that the commerce inside is still prosperous. Certain sorts of shops have, it is true, entirely, or almost entirely, disappeared, partly from the general change of ways of life, partly from the absorption of their business by larger traders. For instance, I believe I am correct in saying that there is not now one single glove-shop left in Paris (I mean a shop in which gloves alone are kept, as used to be the case in former times). The high-class special dealers in lace, in *cachemire* shawls, in silks, have melted away. At the other end of the scale the *herboristes*, who sold medicinal herbs, have vanished too; the *rotisseurs*, who had blazing fires behind their windows, and supplied roast chickens off the spit, have abandoned business; even the hot-chestnut dealer of the winter nights is rarely to be discovered now. Specialities, excepting jewellery, are ceasing to be able to hold their own; emporiums are choking them. Measuring the old shops all round—in showiness, in variety of articles, in extent of business—they were incontestably inferior to those of to-day, though not more so than in any other capital.

The look of the private carriages was also far less bright. They were less well turned out; the horses were heavier; the servants were often badly dressed; the driving was, if possible, more careless. French carriages (like French plates and knives) have always been more lightly made than those of England, and at that time the difference was more marked, because English carriages were more massive than now. The omnibuses and cabs were dirty and uncomfortable; ancient shapes still existed, and, certainly, they did not aid to adorn the streets.

In general terms it may be said that, in Paris, as everywhere else—but more perhaps in Paris than elsewhere—there was, in comparison with to-day, less smartness, less alertness, less hurry, and of course less movement, for the population was much smaller, and the city was still limited by the *octroi* wall. The relative absence of bustle produced, however, no dulness: the streets were not so noisy, not so crowded, not so business-like as they have become since; but I think it is quite true to say that they were as bright.

The brightness came from one special cause, from a spring of action proper to the time, which produced an aspect unlike that of other days. The great peculiarity, the striking mark and badge, which distinguished the streets of then from the streets of now, were supplied by a something which was nationally proper to the

France of the period, by a something which none of us will see at work again in the same form—by the type of the Paris women of the time.

The question of the influence of women on the aspect of out-of-door life has always occupied the attention of travellers. I have discussed it—and, especially, the comparative attractiveness of European women of different races and epochs—with many cosmopolitan observers, including old diplomatists from various lands, who, as a class, are experienced *artistes en femmes* and profound students of "the eternal feminine," and I have found a concordancy of opinion on two points: one, that the women of Paris have always stood first as regards open-air effect (the Viennese are generally put second, though lengths behind); the other, that at no time within living memory have they contributed so largely, so exclusively indeed, to that effect as they did half a century ago. Their performance indoors is not included in the present matter; it is not their talk but their walk, not their home manner but their outdoor *maintien*, not their social action in private but their physical effect in public, that concern us here. Their indoor life is dealt with elsewhere.

The results, to the eye of the passer-by,

were admirable; and so were the processes by
which the results were reached. The period of
Louis Philippe had been essentially honest and
respectable; it had discouraged vanities and
follies; it had encouraged moderation and pru-
dence; it had reacted on the whole organisation
of the life of the time, and, amongst other
things, on women's dress. It was a season
of economy, of frank acceptance of the fruits
of small money, and of an astonishing handiness
in making the most out of little. When we
look back (with the ideas of to-day) to the conditions of expenditure which prevailed then, it
is difficult to believe that, with such limited
resources, the woman of the time can have won
such a place in the admiration of the world.
I am certainly not far wrong in affirming that
the majority of the women of the upper classes
who ambled about the streets in those days had
not spent ten pounds each on their entire toilette
(excepting, of course, the *cachemire* shawl, when
there was one). The tendency of the epoch
was towards extreme refinement, but towards
equally extreme simplicity as the basis of the
refinement. There was no parade of stuffs, or
of colours, or of *façons*; there was scarcely any
costly material; but there was a perfume of

high-breeding and a daintiness of small niceties that were most satisfying to the critical beholder. Finish not flourish, distinction not display, grace not glitter, were the aims pursued. The great ambition—indeed, the one ambition—was to be *comme il faut;* that phrase expressed the perfection of feminine possibilities as the generation understood them. And they were *comme il faut!* Never has delicate femininity reached such a height, never has the ideal "lady" been so consummately achieved. That ideal (by its nature purely conventional) has never been either conceived or worked out identically in all countries simultaneously; local variety has always existed; the Russian lady, the German lady, the English lady, the French lady—I mean, of course, women of social position—have never been precisely like each other: the differences are diminishing with facilities of communication and more frequent contacts, but they still exist perceptibly, and half a century ago were clearly marked. The French lady of the time was most distinctly herself, not the same as the contemporaneous lady of other lands, and the feeling of the judges to whom I have already referred was that, out of doors, she beat them all. I personally remember her

(I was young then, and probably somewhat enthusiastic) as a dream of charm, and feminine beyond anything I have seen or heard of since.

Conceive the effect she produced in the streets! Conceive the sensation of strolling in a crowd in which every woman had done her utmost to be *comme il faut;* in which, as a natural result, a good many looked "born"; in which a fair minority might have carried on their persons the famous lines inscribed on one of the arabesqued walls of the Alhambra, " Look at my elegance; thou wilt reap from it the benefit of a commentary on decoration"! The fashions of the time aided in the production of the effect sought for; they were quiet, simple, subdued; and they were so because the women who adopted them had the good sense to take calm, simplicity, sobriety for their rules.

Alas! the expression *comme il faut* has disappeared from the French language, just as the type and the ideas of which I have been speaking have disappeared from French life. Something very different is wanted now. None but old people know the ancient meaning of *comme il faut;* if the young ones were acquainted with it they would scorn it. As the ' Figaro ' observed some years ago, "la femme comme il faut est

remplacée par la femme comme il en faut."
When the streets were peopled by the· "femme
comme il faut," it was a privilege and a lesson
to walk in them.

And yet, if she could be called to life again,
the streets of to-day would laugh at her. Paris
has grown accustomed to another theory of
woman, and would have no applause to offer
to a revival of the past. The eye addicts itself
to what it sees each day, mistakes mere habit
for reasoned preference, and likes or dislikes,
admires or contemns, by sheer force of contact;
but surely it will be owned, even by those who
are completely under present influences, that
the principles of dress and bearing which were
applied in Paris in the second quarter of the
century had at all events a value which has become rare since. Women attained charm without expense, but with strong personality, for the
reason that they manufactured it for themselves,
and did not ask their tailor to supply it. It was
a delicious pattern while it lasted, and while it
corresponded to the needs of a time; but the
time has passed, the pattern has become anti-
quated, and, in every way, Paris has lost largely
by the change.

Unhappily there was a fault in this attractive

picture; but as it was a fault common to all Europe then, and was in no way special to the French, it did not strike the foreign spectator of those days, because he was accustomed to it everywhere.   The fault was that it was the fashion to look insipid! The portraits of the period testify amply to the fact, for they depict the most expressionless generation that ever had itself painted.   Both ringlets and flat *bandeaux* lent their aid successively to the fabrication of the air of weakness.   The Parisienne, with all her natural vivacity, could not escape from the universal taint: in comparison with what she has been at other times and is to-day, there was about her a feebleness of physiognomy, a suppression of animation, and even, in certain highly developed cases, an intentional assumption of languid vacancy.   But at that time no one perceived this; we were all (men as well as women) determined to give ourselves an appearance of impassiveness, because we regarded it as one of the essential foundations of the *comme il faut*.   We see now how fatuous we looked then; but at the moment we were blind to our own weakness, and simply beheld in placidity of movements and of countenance an indispensable adjunct of distinction.

And yet, with all this putting on of a puerility that did not belong to them, and was in utter contradiction to their nature, I repeat that those women stood entirely apart. Not only had they admirable finish of detail in everything that composed them, but they possessed, furthermore, what they called *la manière de s'en servir*. Their handling of themselves was most interesting to study. What a spectacle it was, for instance, to see one of them come out on a damp day, stop for half a minute beneath the doorway while she picked up her skirts in little gathers in her left hand, draw the bottom tight against the right ankle, and start off, lifting the pleats airily beside her! Both the dexterity of the folding and the lightness of the holding were wonderful to contemplate: no sight in the streets was so intensely Parisian as that one. I imagine that, at this present date, there is not a woman in the place who could do it. The science is forgotten. The putting on of the shawl or mantle was another work of art, so skilfully was it tightened in so as to narrow and slope down the shoulders, as was the fashion then.

And if the higher strata contributed in this degree to the formation of the outdoor picture, almost as much must be said of the share of adornment of the streets which was furnished by many of the women of the lower classes, especially by what still remained of that delightful model, the *grisette*. The *grisette* was dying out at the beginning of the Second Empire, but bright examples of her still survived, and it was impossible to look at them without keen appreciation of their strange attractiveness. It must be remembered that the *grisette* constituted a type, not a class; she was a *grisette* because of what she looked like, not because of what she was. She was rather generally well-behaved, and always hard-working. She was a shop-assistant, a maker of artificial flowers, a sempstress of a hundred sorts, but it was not her occupation that made her a *grisette;* she became one solely by the clothes she chose to put on, and by the *allure* she chose to give herself. The *grisette* of Louis Philippe's time (which was the epoch of her full expansion) wore in the summer—the true season to judge her—a short cotton or muslin dress, always newly ironed, fresh, and crisp; a silk apron; a muslin *fichu;* a white lace cap trimmed with a quantity of flowers; delicate shoes and stockings (buttoned boots for women were just invented, but the *grisette* would have thought herself disgraced for ever if she had come out either in boots or a bonnet); and on Sundays straw kid gloves with the one button of the period. With her sprightly step, the buoyant carriage of her head, her usually slight figure and pretty feet, she lighted up the streets like sunshine, and spread around her an atmosphere of brightness. She had even—in certain cases at all events—a distinction of her own, which was curious and interesting to observe. She, too, did her little best to be *comme il faut*, for that was the rule of the time, and really, in a sort of a way, she sometimes got very near it. Of course, the girls who composed the class of *grisettes* were unequal in their capacities and in the results they achieved. Some grew almost ladylike (though always with a slight savour of what, in Spain, is so expressively called "salt"), while others never lost the look and manners of their origin. But all resisted, with fair success, the influence of surrounding insipidity, and maintained, I think I may say alone, amidst the universal assumption of apathy, the sparkle proper to the Gallic race. Alas! the Haussmannising of Paris gave the last push to the fall of the *grisette*. She vanished with the narrow streets, the paving-stones, and the cheapnesses that had made her possible, and though she lingered for a while, under other names, in some of the provincial towns (especially in Bordeaux, where I saw white caps and flowers as late as 1858), no more was perceived of her in Paris. The damage done to the streets by her disappearance was irremediable: they are almost more changed by it than by all else together.

Of the men of the time I have nothing to say, except that most of them simpered and thought themselves delightful.

The first place was taken by the women, so I have put them first. The second place in the effect of the streets belonged, I think, to the itinerant traders of the moment, most of whom have faded out of being.

The twenty thousand men who lived by keeping the inhabitants supplied with water were certainly the most practically useful of all the vanished workers of that time, and they were omnipresent, for their casks and buckets formed an element of the view in every street. Water was not laid on into the houses; it was carried up each day to every flat, even to the sixth floor, when there was one, by a member of the corporation of the *porteurs d'eau*. Dressed invariably in dark-green or blue velveteen, they tramped heavily and slowly up the staircases, with a load, carried from a shoulder bar, of two great metal pails full to the brim. Worthy fellows they generally were, strong as buffaloes, plodding on an unending treadmill. I often asked myself whether they ever thought. In the streets their casks on wheels (hand-dragged) stood at every door, and children used to watch with delight the perfect unbroken roundness of the arched stream of water which, when the plug was drawn, rushed out of the cask, through a brass-lined hole, into the bucket which stood below it in the roadway. The stream was exactly like a curved staff of glass, and so absolutely smooth that it seemed motionless. The *porteurs d'eau* have gone, like the *grisettes;* they have been replaced by pipes. But while they still existed, while the question of what was to become of them if their work was suppressed was being discussed, the population almost took their side, and, from habit, appeared to prefer the old buckets to the new pipes. Those water-carriers had existed for centuries; they were a component part of the life of Paris; it seemed both cruel and ungrateful to take their bread away, for the sake of a so-called progress which very few persons understood, and of which nobody felt the need; so the philanthropic cried out against the change. I remember being asked to go to a meeting of protestation got up by a lady, who canvassed all her friends. But the buckets were eradicated all the same, only the extinction was effected gradually; the men found other work, and when the community became, at last, acquainted with the advantages of "constant supply," it ceased, thanklessly, to mourn over the giants in velveteen, and wondered, indeed, how it could ever have endured them.

The *chiffonniers*, again, have lost their trade— at least it has become so totally modified that they no longer pursue it in its ancient form. The waste and dirt from every house used to be poured out into the street, before the front door, each evening at nine or ten o'clock, and the *chiffonnier*, with his lantern and his hook in his hands and his basket on his back, arrived at once and raked the heaps over, to see what he could find in them. But it became forbidden either to throw the refuse into the street or to bring it out at night. It was prescribed that it should be carried down in the early morning in a box, which is placed, full, at the door, and is emptied before nine o'clock into the dust-carts which go round each day. The *chiffonniers*, therefore, have no longer the opportunity of picking over the dirt, for it has ceased to offer itself in an accessible form: they have, for the most part, to carry on their trade after the refuse is discharged from the carts at the depots, and, consequently, have almost disappeared from the streets. They cannot be regarded as a loss, for they were, of necessity, dirty and bad smelling, and looked, as they prowled about with their dull lantern in the dark, like spectres of miserable evilness. But, all the same, they were thoroughly typical of old Paris.

There were in those days a quantity of vagrant traders about the streets, *charlatans, marchands ambulants*, and *faiseurs de tours;* the police were merciful to them, and allowed them to carry on their business almost in liberty. Two of them were celebrated: an open-air dentist whose name I have forgotten, and Mangin— "l'illustre Mangin," as he called himself—the pencil-seller. All Paris knew those two. The dentist drove about in a four-wheeled

cart of gorgeous colours, with a platform in
front on which operations were performed.
Immediately behind the platform were an organ
and a drum, which instruments were played,
together or separately, by a boy, and always
irrespectively of each other. Their use was
to drown the yells of the patients. I saw that
dentist frequently at the entrance of the Avenue
Gabriel in the Champs Elysées; but although
there was invariably an excited crowd listening to his eloquence and contemplating his
surgery, I never felt tempted to stop to hear
or watch him, because, with the disposition to
neglect opportunities which is proper to youth,
I failed to see the amusement of staring at
people having their teeth drawn in public. I
am sorry now that I was so fastidious, for I
missed a curious spectacle, and am unable to
describe it here. The show was evidently attractive to a portion of the mob, for there were,
each time I passed, many rows of people applauding the dentist when he declared (in
flowery words, I was assured) that he never
hurt any one, and applauding his victims still
more when they shrieked. I think he charged
five sous (twopence-halfpenny) for dragging out
a tooth; which proves that, as I have already

observed, prices were lower in those days than they are now.

But if I shunned the dentist I never missed a chance of listening to Mangin, who really was a prodigious fellow. It was said that he had taken a university degree, and the varied knowledge which he scattered about in his unceasing speeches gave probability to the rumour. Anyhow, whatever had been his education, his outpour of strange argument, his originality and facility, his spirit of *à propos*, his rapidity of utterance, and, above all, the perpetual newness of his fancies, were positively startling. Of course his talk was often vulgar; but it must be remembered that it was addressed to a street mob, most of whose members loved coarseness. Like the dentist, he paraded about the town in a cart, but his vehicle was dark, and had a high back. Also, like the dentist, he had an organ and a drum, but they were only used in the intervals of his discourses. He had a day and an hour for each quarter of the town, and was always awaited by an eager crowd. The spot where I habitually saw him was in the roadway by the side of the Madeleine. He was then a man of about forty-five, with a great brown beard, pleasant-looking, thick. He wore a huge brass helmet, with immense black feathers, and a scarlet cloak, which he called his toga. His unhesitating command of words, his riotous fertility of subjects and ideas, were such that, though I listened to him frequently, I never heard him make the same observation twice. He did assert continually that he was a descendant of Achilles, and that he wore that gentleman's uniform, but that declaration formed no real part of his speeches; it was a mere official indication, and had in it none of the character of an argument. I think I may say that his harangues were absolutely fresh each day. I do not pretend to remember more than a few of the phrases I have heard him utter, but I can give a fair general idea of his style, including some of his own words. Here is an example :—

Ladies, gentlemen, children, enemies, and friends! —Buy my pencils. There are no other pencils like them on earth or in the spheres. Listen! They are black! You imagine, of course, in the immensity of your ignorance—it is wonderful how ignorant people are capable of being, especially about pencils—that all pencils are black. Error! Criminal error! Error as immense and as fatal as that of Mark Antony when he fell in love with Cleopatra.

All other pencils are grey! Mine alone possess the merit of being truly black. They are black, for instance, as the hair of Eve. Here I pause to observe that it is a general mistake to suppose that Eve was a fair woman. She was as dark as if she had been born in the Sahara, of Sicilian parents. I was in the Garden of Eden with her, and I ought to know. I was, in that stage of my transmigration, the original canary bird, and looked at her as I flew about. I was saying that my pencils are black. Listen! They are black, not only as the hair of Eve, but black as that hideous night after the earthquake of Lisbon; black as the expression of countenance of Alexander the Great (you are aware, of course, that he was an irritable person) when he found there was no sugar in his coffee; black as the waves which gurgled over Phaëthon when he fell headlong into the Po; black as your sweet complexion might be, my dear (to a girl in the crowd), if it did not happen to be, on the contrary, as pink as my toga, as white as my soul, as transparent as the truth of my words. But blackness—friends, enemies, and children—is only one of the ten thousand excellences of my unapproachable pencils. They are also unbreakable, absolutely unbreakable. See! Watch! I dash this finely cut pencil-point on to this block of massive steel. The strength of my arm is such (I inherit it, with other classical peculiarities, from my ancestor, the late Achilles) that I dent the steel; but I cannot break the point. You smile! It wounds me that you smile, for thereby you imply a doubt, just as Solomon smiled while he wondered which of the two women was the mother of the baby. Come up and verify the fact if you do not believe. There is the mark on the steel; there is the pencil-point. The point is sharpened, not blunted, by the fierceness of the blow. One sou, five centimes, for a single pencil! Ten sous, fifty centimes, for a dozen! At those prices I give them away, out of pure love of humanity. Ten sous a dozen! Who buys? Yes, you, sir? Yes. One dozen, or two dozen, or ten dozen? Very good, two dozen. You see, my children, that the entire universe comes to buy my pencils. This gentleman, who has just taken two dozen, has travelled straight from the celebrated island of Jamaica (where humming-birds are cultivated on a vast scale in order to distil from them the sugar they contain) for the express purpose of obtaining a supply. He heard of them out there —I mention for the information of such of you as may not be acquainted with the geography of the oceans, that Jamaica is on the coast of China, and therefore very distant — and he has travelled halfway round the world to come to me to-day. Don't blush, sir, at my revelation of the grandeur of your act. It is a noble act, sir; well may you—and I— be proud of it. Yes, my little beauty, two dozen? You, my child, have not arrived by steamer, railway, or balloon from the celestial waters of Pekin, where the population is born with pigtails, and feeds exclusively on its own finger-nails, which are grown very long for the purpose — you have arrived only from the heights of Montmartre; but your merit also is great, for you have faith in my pencils. Who else has faith in my pencils? Black, unbreakable, easy to cut, easy to suck, easy to pick your teeth with, easy to put behind your ear, easy to carry in your pocket, delightful to make presents with. Who buys my pencils to offer them to her he loves? Yes, young man. Good! Strike the drum, slave; strike the fulminating drum, the very drum that re-sounded at the taking of Troy—it was sent to the relations of Achilles by Ulysses, and has come down as an heirloom in the family—in honour of this noble youth, this brilliant Frenchman, this splendid subject of the Emperor. He offers my pencils to *her!* I drink to *her!* At least I would if I had anything to drink. Ten sous for twelve of such pencils as mine! It's absurd! It pains my heart to sell them. I have to tear myself away from them as the wild horses of Attila tore his prisoners to pieces. The boy who does not buy my pencils is destined to a life of misery; he will be kept in on Sundays; he will be brought up principally on dry bread, but butter and jam will be danced goadingly before his eyes. When he becomes a man he will fail in everything he attempts, and will suffer from many hitherto unknown diseases. His horse, if he has one, will possess a tail like a rolled-up umbrella, and knees the shape of seventy-seven. His cook will put hairs into his soup. As for the girl who does not buy my pencils, her fate will be more

awful still.   Never will she find a husband !   What, girls !
you hear the fearful fate that awaits you, and you do
not rush up instantly to buy ?   Rush, if you wish to be
mothers !   Rush, if you long to be happy, beautiful, and
rich !   That's right ; two, three, four, who long to be
happy, beautiful, and rich.   The more pencils you
buy, the happier, the more beautiful, and the richer
you will be.   How many shall we say ?   Twenty
dozen each ?   I make a reduction for all quantities
over ten dozen.   What ?   One ?   One ?   One single
pencil ?   For one sou ?   And you expect to be
happy, beautiful, and rich for one sou ?   Even in
this glorious land of France, even in this country
of delights, that result is impossible, quite impossible.
Take a dozen at all events ; even then you will only
be relatively happy, moderately beautiful, and not at
all rich.   Joy, loveliness, and wealth increase with
pencils.   Yes, sir, two dozen.   To you, sir, I do
not promise handsomeness, but I predict success,
especially with ladies.   My pencils render men irresistible with women.   Now that you have them in
your hand, try the effect on that tall girl next to
you ; it will be visible at once.   Ten sous a dozen !
Who buys ?   I pause.   I take needed rest, but only
for an instant.   Slave, sound the roaring drum, re-
volve the handle of the pealing organ, in order to
divert the admiring crowd while I repose.

And he proceeded to suck liquorice.

I have given this speech at some length,
because it paints not only a man but a situation.

How utterly other from the conditions of to-day must have been the state of the streets of Paris when it was possible to shout out all that twenty yards from the Boulevard, and to go on shouting every day, without being arrested by the police as a nuisance.

When Mangin disappeared (his eclipse occurred, so far as I can remember, somewhere about 1856) he left vacancy behind him. He was, like Napoleon, unreplaceable.

Another curious artist, of whom I often heard, had gone out of sight before my time. He painted portraits at fairs and in the streets, and a placard at the door of his booth bore in large letters the inscription :—

PORTRAITS !

PORTRAITS !

RESSEMBLANCE FRAPPANTE .	.	2 francs.
RESSEMBLANCE ORDINAIRE .	.	1 franc.
AIR DE FAMILLE . . .	.	50 centimes.

It seems that the *air de famille* was the most largely ordered of the three degrees of likeness, and that scarcely anybody went to the expense of a *ressemblance frappante*. This man made no speeches ; but the wording of his advertisement was worth much talking.

One more exhibitor will I describe—a juggler. He came every Tuesday afternoon to the south-east corner of the Place de la Madeleine, just outside the shop where Flaxland, the music-dealer, is now established; and there, in his shirt-sleeves, he conjured and played tricks. I remember only one of his devices, but that one sufficed to make him a sight of the time. He asked the crowd for pennies (pieces of two sous, I mean); he put five of them into his right hand, played with them, tossed them a few times in the air, and then suddenly flung them straight up to a height which seemed above the house-tops. He watched them intently as they rose, and, as they turned and began to fall, he opened with his left hand the left pocket of his waistcoat, and held it open—about two inches, I should think. Down came the pennies, not loose or separated from each other, but in what looked like a compact mass. Fixedly he gazed at them, shifting his body slightly, very slightly, to keep right under them (he scarcely had to move his feet at all), and crash came the pile into the pocket of his waistcoat! He repeated the operation with ten pennies, and, finally, he did it with twenty! Yes, positively, with twenty! It almost took one's breath away to hear the thud. Never did he miss—at least, never did I see him miss—and never did the pennies break apart or scatter; they stuck to each other by some strange attraction, as if they had become soldered in the air. There was evidently something in the manner of flinging that made them hold steadily together. After wondering each time at the astounding skill of the operation, I always went on to wonder what that waistcoat could be made of, and what that pocket could be lined with, to enable them to support such blows. The force, the dexterity, and the precision of the throwing—to some sixty feet high, so far as I could guess—and the unfailing exactness of the catching, were quite amazing: the pennies went up and came down in an absolutely vertical line. The juggler was said to have made a good deal of money by the proceeding; people talked about it, went to see it, and gave francs to him. He, too, had no successor.

There were plenty of other mountebanks of various sorts about, but they had no widespread reputations, and did not count as recognised constituents of the street-life of the time. Mangin, the dentist, and that juggler held a place amongst the public men of their day—like *Père coupe toujours*, who had sold hot *galette* for half a century in a stall next door to the Gymnase Theatre; like the head-waiter at Bignon's (in the Chaussée d'Antin days, of course), whose name I am ungrateful enough to have forgotten; like the superlatively grand Suisse of that date at the Madeleine, who was said to have been christened Oswald, because the washerwoman, his mother, like many others of her generation, had gone entirely mad over Corinne. How long ago all that does seem! And how utterly other than the Paris of to-day!

The Champs Elysées too—which represented then the concentrated essence of the life of the streets—how changed they are! Then, everybody went there; all classes sat or strolled there. Now, the place is half deserted in comparison with what it was, although the lower part was then a desert of dust or mud, according to the weather, while now it is a real garden; and the upper portion was bordered, at many points, by grass-fields, in which I have seen cows feeding. The planting of the lower half (the trees of course were old) was effected somewhere about 1856, with the stock of a Belgian horticulturist, which was bought *en bloc* for the purpose. It constituted one of the most charming improvements of the Haussmann period, for it gave a look of delightful greenness and prettiness to what had been a gravelly waste. And yet, notwithstanding their beautification, the Champs Elysées, as a public resort, have not maintained the comprehensively representative character they possessed forty years ago. They have been affected partly by the caprices of fashion, but, like all the rest of western Paris, their composition and their aspect have been altered mainly by the almost total separation of the various strata of inhabitants of which I have already spoken. It must be remembered that, in the days of which I am telling, the women of the lower classes were, in great part, ornamental, and that not only were they worthy—many of them, at all events—to take a place in the crowd which assembled every summer evening between the Place de la Concorde and the Rond Point, but that their presence bestowed a special character on the effect of the crowd, for it proved that all the layers of population had learnt to mix naturally together in open-air union. The mixture did not shock the patrician eye, and it pleased the plebeian heart; it did something to soothe and satisfy the self-respect and consciousness of rights of a considerable section of the people, and led them to look with a certain friendliness on the rich. In the Champs Elysées the mingling was more complete even than in the streets, for the double reason that it had more space to show itself, and that the act of sitting down side by side, which was impossible elsewhere, seemed to bestow a certain intimacy on it. Aristocracy lost nothing; democracy gained a good deal; a political effect of utility was achieved.

In those days everything came to pass in the Champs Elysées. Everybody went there to behold everybody else. All processions paraded there—so much so, indeed, that one of the first stories I heard on my arrival in Paris was that, when the end of the world was announced for some day in May 1846, an enterprising speculator set up trestles and planks under the trees, and offered to let out standing-room, at five sous a-head, "to view the end of the world go by." The certainty that everything was to be seen there — from the funeral of the earth to the wedding-party of an oyster-girl going out to dine at a restaurant at Neuilly—was sufficient of course to bring together all the starers of Paris (and there are a good many of them). The true difference between the starers of then

and the starers of now is that in those times the
Champs Elysées were regarded, not only as the
centre of Paris, but as a spot to live in, whereas
now they have become a simple passing place,
like any other—merely one of the ways that lead
to the Bois. The Bois itself was a tangle of
disorder, with few paths in it, and was accessible through a sort of lane turning out of the
present Avenue Victor Hugo, which was then
a narrow road called, if I remember right, the
Route de St Cloud. There was no Avenue du
Bois de Boulogne, nor any other Avenues round
the Arch of Triumph (except, of course, the
Avenue de Neuilly); the Champs Elysées existed alone, and gained naturally in importance
by their oneness. It was not till the late fifties
that the Bois was laid out as it is now, and that
the lakes were dug. When that was done the
world began to go out there, and ceased to stop
in the Champs Elysées.

The Boulevards, again, were far more important features in the life of the place than they
are to-day: then, life was a good deal concentrated; to-day, it is thoroughly spread out. The
building changes which have been effected in the
Boulevards have been enormous, but the modifi-
cations in their social aspect have been greater

still.   Very few of the ancient landmarks survive in them; but the crowd is even more altered than the houses.   The chosen lounging spots are not the same, and even the art of lounging has itself assumed another character.   An acquaintance I made on my first visit to Paris proposed to me seriously to teach me *la manière de flâner*, and spoke of it with reverence, as if it were a science of difficult acquirement, needing delicate attention and prolonged study.   He told me he had passed his life (which had been a long one) in the careful application of the highest principles of lounging, that he had explored its secrets in many countries, and that he had arrived at the conclusion that there are only two capitals where it is carried to its noblest possibilities—Madrid and Paris.   He put Naples third, but with the express reserve that the lounging there is simply animal, and has no elevation in its composition.   He did admit, however, that in Madrid and Naples the entire population knows instinctively how to lounge, while in Paris the faculty is limited to the educated.   To-day it is in Paris itself that the lounging has lost "elevation"; it has become as "animal" as at Naples, but without the excuse of the sun which, there, bestows so much justification on its animality. Parisians no longer lounge with the sublime contentment which was so essentially characteristic of the process forty years ago. In those days the mere fact of being on the Boulevard sufficed not only to fill the true *flâneur* with a soft religious joy, but aroused in him a highly conscious sentiment of responsibility and dignity: he seemed, as he strolled along, to be sacrificing to the gods. Alas! it is the mere material act of lounging, without adoration for the sacred place where the act is performed, which satisfies the actual mind. The distinction between the two conditions, between the "elevation" of the one and the "animality" of the other, is self-evident and lamentable. If my old friend were not dead already, the sight, assuredly, would kill him. He declared—and it was an opinion generally held then—that, for a true Parisian, the only portion of the Boulevard which was really fit for the due discharge of the holy duty of lounging was the little space between the Rue du Helder and the Rue Lepelletier, which, with fond memories of other days, he persisted in calling by its former momentary name of "Boulevard de Gand" (for the reason that, during the Hundred Days, Louis XVIII. ran away to

Gand). The bottom of the steps of Tortoni formed the hallowed central spot. When I first saw Paris, that spot inspired me, under the guidance of my old friend, with a certain awe; but I must add that the awe did not last, and that the more I knew of the spot the less I revered it.

It has been said of French Governments that "plus ça change, plus c'est la même chose;" but, however true that may be of Ministries, it is absolutely untrue of outdoor Paris, which has altered so totally that it has ceased to be the same at all. Perhaps it might be a good thing for France if the Government were to change as completely.

CHAPTER II.

I WAS crossing the Place de la Concorde, thinking of nothing, when suddenly I became aware that carriages, accompanied by a small crowd, were advancing slowly towards me from the Avenue Gabriel.   The marriage of Napoleon III. with Mademoiselle de Montijo was to be solemnised that day in the Cathedral of Nôtre Dame.   The carriages I saw coming formed the procession of the bride.

I placed myself at the edge of the pavement, on the west side of the obelisk, just where the guillotine stood during the Terror, and looked.

Almost at a foot's pace the carriages drove past me, two yards off.   In one of them, which seemed to be all glass, I caught sight of an intensely pale, intensely anxious face.   I presume there were surroundings; there may have

been white satin, orange flowers, jewels; there
may have been other persons: but I saw absolutely nothing—and was capable of seeing nothing
—except the absorbing presence of those dream-
ily apprehensive eyes and those pallid cheeks.
That expression of vague heart-sinking blotted
out every detail of attendant circumstances;
it left no room in me for any other perception
whatever.

As I gazed the vision vanished; it had endured for only a dozen seconds, and yet it had
stamped itself permanently inside my head;
it has remained there, clear, sharp, abiding.
I have seen that face often since,—in youth, in
age; in pride, in pain; illumined by the glitter
of a meteoric throne, worn by disaster, grief, and
exile,—but never have I looked at it without
the accompanying memory of its almost spectral
apparition to me on 29th January 1853.

I was told next day (by enemies of the Empire)
that Mademoiselle de Montijo expected to be
assassinated on her way to church, and that
the expression I had observed was the natural
consequence of the alarm she felt. But I protested against that explanation. I felt instinctively that I had beheld something else than
mere material fear, something other than simple

dread of the present. At the moment, it is true, I regarded the expression of that face merely as an involuntary testimony to the vanity of success; I had then no motive for attributing to it any other meaning. In later days, however, it assumed to me the very different aspect of a revelation of failure. Looking back to it now, as it floated past me forty-two years ago, on the exact spot where Marie Antoinette was executed, I discern what I believe was really in it—awe of the future, augury of woe.

I have forgotten many other sights, but that one stands vividly before me in its sadness. To me the recollection of it means that, at the very moment when the ex-Empress was on her way to Nôtre Dame to put on a crown, I chanced to see her sorrows foreshadowed to her.

CHAPTER III.

UNDER the Second Empire the balls at the Hôtel de Ville counted amongst the bright festivities of Europe. Sovereigns, society, the many foreigners in Paris, the upper *employés* of the Municipality, and *le haut commerce* met at them; they were admirably done; the great gallery was magnificent; everybody who possessed a uniform wore it; the show was very brilliant, and, notwithstanding the extreme variety of guests, scarcely anybody looked ugly. Nowhere could there be found a more interesting exhibition of intermingled classes, more creditable manners on the part of the unaccustomed portions of the invited, more cordial acceptance of momentary mixture on the part of the rest. Those balls supplied special occasions for contemplating groupings of very diversified social categories and of very various nationalities, all in their best clothes.   There was no political character about them, nor did they present any popular peculiarities in the ordinary meaning of the word ; but they were as royal, aristocratic, and international as they were commercial, bureaucratic, and French.   Nearly all the monarchs and princes of the time—and their wives and daughters too — showed themselves successively in that gallery, and every land was represented in it by notable men and women.

The ball of 22d August 1855, at which Queen Victoria and Prince Albert were present, may fairly be taken as a typical example.   It was not different from the others, but it was as good as any of them, and it presented, in their fullest degree, all the special characteristics of the gatherings at the Hôtel de Ville.   I do not remember with any exactness what happened at it, for each *fête* was so like the others that they have run into a confused blend in my recollection ; but errors, if I make them, will be of no importance as regards effect and outline, for whatever was true of one ball was true of another, if not specifically, at all events generically.

The ride to the Hôtel de Ville was wearisome. The *queue* of carriages began at the Place de la Concorde, and the invited had to go on thence at a foot's pace for at least an hour, with the irritation of seeing the possessors of a *coupe file* drive straight on at a trot. I explain that a *coupe file* is a card given each year by the Paris police to official persons, to enable them on all occasions to go on unstopped to their destinations. The result was that the immense majority disembarked at last in an ill-temper.

After passing through the splendid inner court, where, under the arch of the grand staircase, was the famous transparent cascade—the water rippling, trickling, splashing down high steps of deadened glass lighted brightly from behind, amidst masses of variegated plants and hanging flowers — the crowd marched up the broad ascent, lined with soldiers at attention. At the top, on the great landing, it found itself face to face with the givers of the ball, the Municipal Council and the Prefect of the Seine, who, with a forest of palm-trees behind them, stood there to receive their arriving visitors. And on that landing there was a curious little sight to see.

The Council, which in those days was nominated by the Government, not elected by the local Radicals as it is now, formed a semicircle (forty of them, when they were all there). They had a uniform of their own, proper to themselves; it was, if I remember rightly, brown embroidered with silver; the Prefect in the middle with a coat of another colour, to show, I presume, that he was governmental, not municipal. The entire party bowed, collectively, cohesively, and concentrically, though with irregularities of inflexion, to every person who appeared; and, as people poured up-stairs in an unceasing mob, the bowing kept the brown uniforms in a condition of permanent oscillation, at the rate, I should imagine, of about fifteen bows a minute. It was a very creditable gymnastic performance, especially as most of the forty acrobats were decidedly old, and all eminently respectable well-to-do gentlemen of solid position, — bankers, manufacturers, professors. That side of the process constituted a feature in itself, and was alone worth going to one of the balls to behold. But the return bows of the entering crowd were immeasurably more remarkable. I think, indeed, that they presented the most striking specimens of unfortunate salutations that it has been given me to view. The operation had to be performed with extreme rapidity because of the pressure from behind, so that all that could usually be managed by most people was to curve hurriedly towards some vague point of the crescent, which was only visible to ordinary eyes as a suddenly appearing and very indistinct chocolate line, and leave the rest unnoticed. But this insufficient solution did not satisfy the more earnest and less experienced section of the guests; they thought it was their stern duty to try to deliver their bow rotatorily, so as to include the entire arc in the manifestation of respect. Now an elliptically-shaped salute addressed to about seventy feet of brown coats, with or without a glance to each of them, cannot be completed under fifteen seconds at the lowest computation, and never were fifteen seconds allowed to any one for the purpose. The executant was invariably upset by a push from somewhere, tumbled over his own legs, and staggered away humiliated, recognising that he had attempted more than it was in his power to get through with either grace or safety. The women managed better than the men; their little curtsies, though rapid, were often well achieved. Some people, women as well as men, marched nobly past the brown-and-silver coats without taking the slightest notice of them, which, though ungrateful, was very practical and perhaps partially excusable.

When the Imperial and Royal guests arrived (which was always rather late, so as to allow time for the ordinary public to get in first), the Prefect and the Council went down to meet them at the door, and of course from that moment there was no more bowing; for which reason timid persons, who feared the operation on the landing, started late, so as not to reach the ball until the Royalties were in. People looked somewhat at the sovereigns when they entered; but, for two reasons, staring of that sort is relatively little practised in Paris. The first reason is, that the French, taken as a nation and not counting the individual exceptions, have learned that Royal personages are not different from themselves; the second, that snobbishness in France has but slight national existence,—it is to be found in society, but not amongst the masses, and even in society there is comparatively little disposition to glare at monarchs. It must be remembered, in explanation of this, that there is no nationally recognised upper class, as in England, to admire, to imitate, and to attain.

The sovereigns took their place on a dais in the middle of one side of the great gallery (when there happened to be no sovereigns that dais was occupied by the notabilities of the evening, whoever they might happen to be). They sat there in pre-eminence until the moment came for the procession through the rooms. Scarcely any one followed them in their walk, except the Court and the official people; they were left in such peace as is accessible to Royalty. There was, however, a curiosity to see Queen Victoria; indeed, she was more looked at, with the single exception of the Emperor of Russia in 1867, than any other royal visitor to Paris in my time. The English were, strange to say, rather popular in France just then (it was during the alliance of the Crimean war). Her Majesty was the only English reigning sovereign who had ever come to Paris; she was a woman; her presence was regarded as an act of high courtesy and as of good augury.

The Emperor and Empress and their guests left early; but their departure produced no effect upon the ball; it went on as before. There was no Court etiquette, no rules of special behaviour towards monarchs any more

than towards other people; all that was expected was that the latter would be respectful
towards the former.   The only difference after
they had withdrawn was that, the slight dis-
traction of Royal presence having ceased, the
crowd was able to bestow its exclusive attention
on what was, undeniably, and in everybody's
opinion, the most marked national characteristic of the Hôtel de Ville balls.   That characteristic was the show of uniforms.

Never anywhere was there brought together
such a prodigious variety of many - shaped,
many-coloured, and much-embroidered coats.
Nearly all the presentable male costumes of
the world must have appeared at one or other
of those balls; everybody, from all parts of
the earth, came to Paris in those days; everybody went to the Hôtel de Ville; everybody,
as I have already said, wore a uniform if he
had one, and on the Continent all functionaries
possess raiments distinctive of their office.   No
Court assemblage supplied, or does supply, such
a varied pageant, for the simple but decisive
reason that, with the exception of the diplomatic body, very few foreigners are to be seen
at Courts.   At the Hôtel de Ville of Paris,
on the contrary, the gathering was extraordin-

arily cosmopolitan. It included specimens of everybody from everywhere, and presented a collection of male attire of which nobody has seen the like before or since.

I often heard discussions as to the relative effect produced by each one of the hundreds of diversified equipments, and I remember that the common verdict gave the front place to the uniform of the Hussar generals of the Austrian army (the same opinion has been expressed about it wherever else I have encountered it). The tunic and breeches are scarlet, embroidered abundantly with gold; the dolman white, laced with gold and edged with sable; the busby is in sable. Nothing more superb has been imagined,. thus far, as a covering for man. At St Petersburg there is an amazing exhibition of Asiatic uniforms, some of them most resplendent and effective; yet when they are transplanted into Western Europe they lose the naturalness they possess in Russia, do not produce the same effect of being in their right place, and assume a more or less barbaric aspect. But that Austrian uniform preserves the same distinguished character wherever it is beheld. Many of the civil uniforms were bright and well conceived, especially the fifteen or twenty sorts of them that were worn by the divers officials of the Imperial Court; but, as a rule, in that exhibition the soldiers had certainly the best of the clothes. I was much diverted at the Queen's ball (at least I believe it was at that one) by the agitating sensation provoked by a kilted High-lander. Wherever he went a mob accompanied him, looking gapingly but disapprovingly at his legs, and wondering whether the police would turn him out for impropriety. The women in particular were curious to see him, but shocked when they did so; they crowded up to him, gazed, and then retired discreetly. He had undeniably the success of the evening, so far, that is, as bewildered staring can be said to constitute success.

The mass of other caparisons dwells as a promiscuous fog in my memory. I can describe none of them. I remember only and vaguely that every hue was represented; that, for in-stance, there were at least fifteen competing shades of red, from the pink burnoose of a Morocco sheikh, through all the hues of scarlet, crimson, and amaranth, to the dark claret of the Empress's chamberlains. But, misty as is my recollection of details, I can repeat with

certainty that the display, as a whole, constituted a prodigious glitter, and that there was
ample justification for the popular impression
that the uniforms were always the particular
show of those balls.

And yet there was in the air around those
coats the inevitable sensation (inevitable because it is felt on every occasion when such coats
are looked at) that the clothes blotted out the
man. The wearer needs to look particularly
some one if he is to succeed in maintaining
his personality in spite of obtrusive trappings.
Colours, gold lace, stars, ribbons, and other
varied glories, assert themselves at the expense
of the body within them; even that admirable
Austrian uniform requires a wearer as smart
as his clothes if he is to avoid being effaced
by them. Our eye is caught by the outside;
the inside is relatively invisible. When, under
such circumstances, we look for the inside, we
have sometimes difficulty in perceiving any inside at all. The black clothes of every night,
hideous as they are, have at all events the
merit, by their uncompeting dulness, of leaving
the individual in full visibility; but uniform is
always more or less disguising and produces
the contrary result; and the more magnificent

the uniform, the more contrary is the result, which is wounding for the vanity of mankind. Shabby clothes obliterate a man in one direction; smart ones obliterate him in another.

By the side of the men the women at those balls lost their usual supremacy of effect. They were simply what they always were, in evening dresses; they offered no special spectacle; the men supplied that all by themselves. We were accustomed to see women *décolletées*, but we were not accustomed to see such a mass of men from all parts of the world in their gala costumes. The effect of uniforms must indeed have been vigorous to deaden, as it did most assuredly at those strangely intermingled balls, the counter-attraction of women.

An amusing particularity of those composite festivals was that they supplied occasions, which were rarely found otherwise, for foreigners to get introduced to a few French people, and I think the French rejoiced in the accident even more than the foreigners. A French girl was not inconsiderably flattered to find one of the gorgeous strangers, whom she had been contemplating with an admiration approaching to awe, brought up to her as a candidate for a dance. Whether he was an officer of Spanish halberdiers, a black Brunswicker, a Hungarian in velvet, a Zeithen hussar, a Papal Noble Guard, or a Danish Secretary of Legation in scarlet (the Danes are the only diplomatists who wear red), he was equally curious to her, and equally welcome. I cannot say if she would have had the courage to stand up with a Highlander; I doubt it. I have heard pleased talk in French families of the acquaintances made in those days at the Hôtel de Ville. Often were mothers graciously pleased to observe : " It is extraordinary; but really some of these foreigners are very agreeable, and their get-up is superb. In France we have no uniforms like theirs."

It is scarcely to be expected that such balls will ever be seen again. They were only rendered possible by the combination of the peculiar conditions of life under the Second Empire with the momentary absence of all international hates. They were a product of circumstances which have passed away with the period which begot them, and which, from the present look of things, do not seem likely to return. The whole civilised world was anxious to come to them; for while they offended no opinions and shocked no prejudices, they pleased even the most experienced eyes, and to beginners seemed incredibly brilliant. On looking back to other festivities at which I have assisted in many lands, I unhesitatingly put first those balls at the Hôtel de Ville of Paris, and I consider it a privilege to have seen them and to have the memory of them. They did not offer, of course, the stately ceremonial or the finished pageantry of balls at the great Courts, but they were far more generally representative, and far more widely cosmopolitan, than any of the *fêtes* that are usually seen in palaces.

Since those days I have been present at one more ball at the Hôtel de Ville. Not in the same building, alas! for it was burnt in the Commune of 1871, but in the new edifice which has been built since on the same site, and in which the actual Municipal Council has given a certain number of entertainments to its electors. After much hesitation I was induced to go to one of them on the 2d of April 1887, and I have never ceased to regret that I was weak enough to yield to the pressure of the friends who urged me to accompany them.

I will not attempt to describe what I beheld; all I will say is that there is not one single point in common between the balls of then and the balls of now,—save the fact that both are technically described by the same title of "Balls at the Hôtel de Ville." It would be both pitiful and ridiculous to give an exact account of the present after what I have been saying of the past.

Neither society nor foreigners were to be seen at the new ball, and, excepting a few French officers, there was not a single man in uniform. The type of the visitors was so utterly altered that I stood wondering how it was possible that mere changes of political circumstances could have brought about so prodigious a transformation. The simple substitution of the Republic for the Empire was not sufficient to explain it, for though strangers no longer come to Paris, there are still delightful-looking French people in quantities. The true causes of the revolution are the transfer of municipal authority to an intensely radical body, to the consequent introduction of a totally new category of guests, and to the absence of all persons of social position who, even if they were invited, would refuse to go. I came away at the end of half an hour with a feeling of something like disgust, but with the consolation of recognising that the strange sight at which I had been glancing had

not affected my impressions of other days;
that those impressions, notwithstanding what
I had just seen, remained unweakened; and that
neither the brilliancy of their old colouring nor
the clearness of their old outlines had been
affected by the terrible contrast of the spectacle
which claims nominally to replace them.

To the Radicals of to-day a "ball at the
Hôtel de Ville" may mean such a gathering as
I was led to on 2d April 1887, but to the world
at large it still signifies, and probably will always signify, a ball of the Imperial period.

CHAPTER IV.

THE LAST DAY OF THE EMPIRE.

THE story of the 4th of September 1870 has been told so often and so minutely that it would be useless to relate it again for itself; there is nothing left to tell. Furthermore, my own recollections of it are very slight, for I beheld almost nothing of what happened. Like other people, I have read up the tale since, but I am only acquainted with the greater part of it at second hand. If I speak of the day here, it is not, therefore, because I have any particular knowledge of its details, but for the totally different reason that it produced in me a tremendous sensation of ruin which I have never forgotten, and which has placed it in the very front of my memories of Paris. Of that sensation alone have I anything to say.

The period before Sedan had been leadenly

oppressing. The air was full of a constantly augmenting sickly apprehension. The "light heart" with which the war began had utterly disappeared. The battles round Metz had crushed out the optimism of the French ; alarm had taken root and grown; the possibility of complete defeat was, so far, admitted by no one ; the yearning to conquer was passionate, poignant, convulsive; but there had crawled into every mind a wearying strain, a restless quivering, an undefined fearfulness of the future, which were reflected in almost every face. To make matters still more painful, it was felt that, amidst that terrible anxiety, the news supplied was unreliable : the daily statements in the papers were more or less fantastic and conflicting; even the official telegrams posted up at the Ministry of the Interior in the Place Beauvau were regarded with suspicion. The struggle between gnawing fear and desperately persistent hope, between the new crushing evidence of facts and the old deeply-rooted national conviction that France could not be beaten, was cruelly fierce.

The position of foreigners had become difficult. It was scarcely possible for a stranger, whatever were the reality and the strength of his sympathies for France, to view the situation as the French did. Every single Frenchman with whom I talked during those gloomy days was convinced that the successes of the Prussians were due to "treachery," though nobody defined, or attempted to define, the meaning or the application of the word; and, additionally, every one insisted that it was the duty of every other country to take the side of France. How could a foreigner agree with such ideas? And yet it was essential to put on an appearance of agreement with them in order to avoid quarrels: it was not permitted to be neutral; it was obligatory to talk in the same tone as the French under penalty of being regarded by them as an enemy. This made the situation infinitely disagreeable; but there is no denying that, all the same, notwithstanding its inconveniences and risks, it was even more infinitely interesting.

I was surrounded by a confused mixture of "patriotic anguish" (the phrase was first used by M. Rouher), of fanatical suspicions, of gasping longings for victory, of chafing rage against the monstrous injustice of fate and against the perfidious indifference of other nations. All tempers were worried, fractious, querulous. I had before me the spectacle of a nation heart-sick.

Such was the general state of mind in which Paris reached Saturday the 3d of September. The battle of Sedan had been fought two days before; but though it appears certain, from evidence produced since, that the Government was acquainted with the issue on the night of the 2d, it was not till the morning of the 3d that private telegrams from London and Brussels brought the first rumours of a great reverse; not till four in the afternoon that the lamentable despatch to the Empress arrived—

L'armée est defaite et captive; moi-même je suis prisonnier.   NAPOLÉON.

—not till seven in the evening that the whole awful news burst out.

I had been ill that day and had been obliged to stay indoors. No one had come to see me, which was natural, for most of my acquaintances had left Paris. I cannot, however, pretend that I regretted their absence, because, for the reasons I have just given, I had begun to shrink somewhat from seeing French friends. The result was that I learned nothing on the Saturday night, and went to bed before sunset, unwell and anxious, but ignorant.

On the Sunday morning a servant woke me with the news of Sedan, which had been raging over Paris for twelve hours without my knowing one word about it. It scared me utterly. A feeling dashed into me that there was an end of France. It came with a devastating rush; no reasoning led me to it; it was there — in me. I had expected disaster, but not such disaster as that. The reality surpassed all imagination. There seemed suddenly to be nothing left. The Emperor and his whole army taken! Never shall I forget the desolating alarm for France that seized me. Of course it was exaggerated (especially when looked at from this distance and under present conditions). Of course, if I had been able to think coolly, and had given myself time to do it, I should have recognised that France herself existed still; but, under the pulverising circumstances of the moment, I really think I had some cause for that first impression. The blow seemed more and more stunning as each second passed. I had not conceived that political demolition could produce an even greater moral effect than material destruction.

I read the papers throbbingly, rolled about in bed, stared blankly and blackly at the future, and passed through a strangely painful quarter of an hour.

Then, naturally, my ordinary ways reasserted themselves, and, though I was still ill, I got up to dress, go out, and see what was happening.

The instant I was outside my door I was conscious of a change in the aspect of Paris. Something had come into it since the day before. The atmosphere was other. My street (which, though wide enough for a great thoroughfare, led to nowhere in particular and was usually empty) was not calm; groups, unknown in ordinary life, stood about in it, discussing, disputing, gesticulating. In the nearest gathering I perceived a *concierge* I knew, so I stopped and asked him—

"What are people saying?"

"Oh, all sorts of things," he answered, incoherently; "some talk one way and some another; some pity the Emperor; some say he has betrayed us and has sold us to William, and that it serves him right to be caught himself; some think the Prussians will be in Paris to-morrow, and that we shall all be prisoners."

"And what is going to happen to-day?" I inquired.

Instead of replying, my acquaintance looked timidly round the circle, leaving it to one of the others to mutter savagely—

"They are coming down from Belleville; there will be a fight on the Boulevard, and there will be no Empire left to-night. Curse the Emperor!"

Not one of them had a word for France! They had apparently but two subjects of thought — themselves and the Emperor; the country did not seem to count.

In the next street, where there was more movement, there was also more bitterness; the people were still mainly of the same class, peaceful folks, above the position of artisans, with interests to protect, habitually stagnant, not revolutionary, not politicians, still less soldiers, accustomed to leave everything to the Government; but that morning there was a heaving amongst them of which I should not have imagined them capable. There were visibly increasing sneerings at the Emperor, there were rejoicings over his fall; but, nevertheless, there were still many in the streets during those first hours of the day who were only softly sad, and who had the courage to say they pitied him. It was not until the afternoon that the entire population, under the influence of events and of example, turned unanimously against him and poured out universal imprecations on his name. I noticed again and again, and everywhere, that no one spoke of France. I appeared to be alone in my intense preoccupation about her future, and I well remember the feeling of strange solitude I experienced in those crowds, where, so far as I could judge from the signs on the surface, no one seemed to share my anxiety for the country herself. Perhaps it was precisely because, not being directly concerned, I was able to view the situation as a whole more easily than the French could.

Not an allusion was made to the Empress. She was not liked. At that moment of supreme distress no one, within my hearing, manifested any interest in her, or any care as to what might become of her.

I went slowly on from street to street, joining often in the groups, listening to the talk, observing always the same contradictory symptoms, the same compound of relatively peaceful distress, of comparatively tranquil irritation, and of profound personal disquietude, with an ever-enlarging proportion of ferocity and of cries for vengeance against Napoleon III.

At the entrance to the Grand Hotel I met two acquaintances, both terribly depressed, both certain that, notwithstanding the position of France, the Emperor would be dethroned at once, both utterly indifferent to the political future. It was not their business to form another Government, and they said they did not care what Government came in provided only it could beat the Prussians. For that one result they did sigh passionately; but their longings did not appear to extend further. When I ventured to suggest that it was not quite the moment to effect a revolution, and that such work as that had better be left until the enemy was no longer looking on, they replied that they did not care, provided only some one would win a battle. At the moment I thought their tone and attitude special to themselves, but afterwards I had reason to suppose that they represented fairly well the condition of opinion of a large portion of the educated classes. Nearly all of them had lost sight of every consideration save victory alone.

They told me that, in all probability, the mob from Belleville and the National Guards from everywhere, would not reach the Chamber until one or two o'clock, and that nothing riotous could be expected until then. So, as I was weak and tired, and as I had satisfied my immediate longing for contact with outside news and outside impressions, I thought I had had enough. My sensations (which I. remember vividly) formed a confused jumble of horror of the realities of the instant, of extreme distress for France, of wondering anxiety as to what would happen next, and of a beginning of hesitation as to what I had better do. For the first time I asked myself whether, under the new circumstances which surrounded me, it was either worth while or wise for me to stop on in Paris. I was catching from the French some share of their preoccupation about their individual fates.

Sadly I smouldered homewards. I determined not to look on at the coming catastrophe. I was not tempted to see history of that sort made. I had always gone to view sights, no matter of what nature. The disposition to be an eye-witness of everything that happened had been strong in me; but on that 4th of September I shrank from the spectacle of destruction, for I fancied I could hear the German armies laughing with delight at the work French hands were performing at such a moment and under such conditions. I determined to shut my eyes, wilfully, in order not to see. I could not face the smash, for it meant, as I judged it under the impressions of the instant, the irreparable fall of France.

Yet after lunch the old habit thrust itself forward again, and notwithstanding my illness and my repugnance, I dragged myself back miserably to the Boulevard. In my then state of mind these fluctuations of feeling and of action appeared to me quite natural.

It was about four o'clock when I reached the top of the Rue de la Paix, just in time to see the return of a part of the crowd which had been urging on the National Guards to attack the Chamber. I heard from eager mouths around me that a Government of lawyers was to be proclaimed at the Hôtel de Ville. The mob yelled frantically as it marched on; the weather was superbly fine; that such a scene of national disgrace (as I regarded it) should be enlustred by so gorgeous a daylight appeared to me to be a desecration of the sun. The sight before me was politically and morally so dismal that I could not pardon the sky for shining on it.

That the Empire should be turned out with dishonour was inevitable, necessary, and just; but not while fighting was going on, not on the morrow of a vast defeat. The sentence on it should have been pronounced at another and a fitter moment. The stream that France was wading through was too wide, too muddy, and too flooded for her to stop to swop horses in the middle of it. I could not forgive the half-dozen deputies who on such a day thought fit to seize the Government for their own use. I cared nothing for the Empire, but that it should be kicked off by the French themselves under the blows and before the eyes of the victorious enemy, appeared to me to constitute a still further fall for France. The demerits of the Empire did not exculpate those who made the unpatriotic revolution of the 4th of September. The arraignment of the Empire should have been reserved until the last German had left the soil. How infinitely more solemn it would have become! And assuredly there is no reason for supposing that the war would have been continued either less vigorously or more unsuccessfully.

The mob kept pouring on, tumultuous, delighted, as if it had performed a noble act. I was told that it varied its pastimes by occasionally hunting down "a spy," but I saw nothing of the process. It is true I was half-dazed and beheld dimly. The destinies of France had become dear to me from long contact with her, and I was possessed by an extraordinarily intense perception of her ruin. I was in `a waking nightmare of wreckage, crashing, and annihilation. I could not have supposed it possible to get face to face with such a sentiment of havoc and outrage.

There was additionally, since that morning, the new sudden fear that Paris would be besieged! Nobody, so far, had thought of that as a realisable possibility. Paris besieged! The capital of the earth beleaguered! "*La ville lumière*" dragged down to the level of a mere fortress and invested! Where was the world going when such a thing could be?

That was, however, the future, the near future perhaps, but still the future. The present was sufficient in itself; the present was Sedan, the disappearance of the Empire in the gutter, and the triumph of the Radical barristers. I wished to look no further for the moment.

I longed to be alone. The crowd, the shouts, the seizure of power by a faction in consequence of a national defeat, and, almost more than all, the wanton, remorseless, mocking sunlight, staring blazingly at the scene as if it approved and applauded, offended me to the bottom of my heart. It was a time for mourning, not for noise; for sadness, not for glare.

The moral impression of which I have not ceased to speak hung massively upon me. I turned away into back‑streets, where there were shadows in harmony with my thoughts. I crawled home, laid down, and felt wretched. I knew, at last, what it is to see a nation sink.

CHAPTER V.

THE ENGLISH FOOD GIFTS AFTER THE SIEGE.

WHEN the siege of Paris was drawing to its
end, and when lamentable reports of the starvation that was going on inside were circu-
lating about Europe, everybody took it for
granted that, for a time after the opening of
the gates and until regular supplies could be
obtained once more, a considerable portion of
the population would continue to be in serious
straits for food. The stocks in the place were
known to be exhausted; the railways had been
much damaged, and required to be got back
into working condition before traffic could be
reorganised and provisions brought in; and it
was imagined, additionally, that a good many
people would have no money to pay for bread.
For these various reasons it seemed certain
to outsiders that a period of serious want would

have to be bridged over. The gaze of the
world was fixed on Paris; everybody felt personal sorrow for it; the deepest interest in the
griefs of its inhabitants was everywhere expressed. In England, as elsewhere, the talk
of the time was full of sympathy; and in England—though not elsewhere—active measures
were taken to show the reality of that sympathy.
The Lord Mayor of London called a meeting
at the Mansion House, as he usually does
when a great suffering claims alleviation, appealed to the British public to help Paris, and
opened a subscription. With the product of
that subscription (which was large), food was
bought in quantities in anticipation of the surrender, and was sent off to Havre and Dieppe,
in the hope that, by effort and good luck, it
might, somehow, be got up to Paris in time
to be of use.

The situation appeared to be made worse
still by one of the conditions of the capitulation, which stipulated that no food for Paris
should be drawn from any of the portions of
France then occupied by the Germans,—the
reason being that the conquerors needed for
themselves all that those portions could produce. This restriction signified that, as all

the Northern Departments, up to the Belgian frontier, were in German hands, and as German regiments had stretched out beyond Normandy in the west, and beyond Burgundy in the south, supplies for the capital could only be practically sought in distant departments. But the Germans, very generously, did not enforce this clause, and allowed food to be bought for Paris wherever it could be found, even at Versailles, where they really required it for their own people. The result was that, as the railways were patched up wonderfully fast, stocks got in with a relative abundance and a positive speed which astonished the beholders.

It happened in reality, after all this apprehension, that Paris had scarcely starved at all, in the strict sense of the term. Everybody who had money to spend was able, throughout the siege, to obtain necessaries in sufficient quantity, and even certain luxuries. The starvation that was so much talked of by commiserating Europe rarely meant, for the mass of the population, any absolute absence of food. I did not hear of one proved case of death from hunger; but, of course, I do not pretend that none occurred, for, even in ordinary times, people in large agglomerations die frequently from want. Throughout the siege, too, charity was at work with open hands; the richer people contributed abundantly to the relief of the needs around them. There was discomfort for the wealthy; there was scantiness for the middle classes; there was privation for the poor; all sorts of unaccustomed nourishment were utilised; but there was always food of some sort, though generally inferior in quality, and in many cases insufficient in quantity. A certain number of persons, especially women, had, towards the end, great difficulty in obtaining bread at all, because at that time it had to be fetched, with tickets, from the bakers' shops—a process which involved hours of waiting in the cold. Various forms of dyspepsia, and even of organic diseases, were brought on by bad eating; inflammations of the chest were numerous; but, so far as I could learn on the spot (and I took a great deal of trouble to inquire, at the time), most of the damage done was to persons of previous weak health. I must say, also, that the consequences did not always manifest themselves at once,—in many cases they appeared months afterwards; deaths from illnesses caused by the siege were heard of -more frequently perhaps in 1872 than in

1871. The men were better off than the women, because, during the whole duration of the investment, nearly all of them could get two francs a-day as National Guards, while the women could earn nothing, and suffered, consequently, more. There were, of course, many cases of exceptional distress; many persons were unable to digest, or even to swallow, the abominable bread that was supplied to the public during the concluding weeks (those who could afford it did their baking at home with flour they had laid up at the beginning, or else ate rice instead of bread): of course the scarcity of fuel and the bitter cold of the winter of 1870 added to the suffering; but that suffering, though occasionally intense, was not universal, and, especially, it never presented the character of true siege famine. Another fortnight would have produced that famine; but the capitulation was signed in time, and, taking the population as a whole and putting aside the exceptions, Paris went through only the earliest stages of the consequences of a prolonged investment. Occasional instances of acute misery cannot be counted for anything under such circumstances and amidst so vast a population. Considering what war really is, what it really means, and what it may entail, Paris made scarcely any acquaintance with its limitless horrors. There was a good deal of illness, but no general starvation properly so-called. For a city of brightness and pleasure the trial was very painful and humiliating; but for a beleaguered fortress it could scarcely be regarded as a true siege. As a moral and material hardship inflicted suddenly on people who had always lived in *insouciance*, the imprisonment was extremely worrying and painful; but as a military operation, involving possibly all the frightful followings of battle, it induced, comparatively, very few woes at all. The situation might have been so immeasurably worse than it was, that it cannot be regarded as having been thoroughly bad.

At the immediate moment, however, nothing of this truth was known; the facts only came out by slow degrees. The exact contrary, indeed, was believed outside. And that was why the world wept for Paris, and why the English of the period desired to aid in mitigating her sorrows.

The capitulation and the armistice were signed about 27th January, and on 4th February (if I remember correctly) Colonel Stuart

Wortley and Mr George Moore arrived in Paris as delegates of the Lord Mayor's Committee, bringing with them a first small supply of stores. They set themselves at once to prepare for the distribution of " the English gifts " that were following them, formed a Paris Committee to help in the work, and were good enough to ask me to join it. I had just come in from Versailles, where I had passed the siege time: I was very curious to see with my own eyes the state of Paris, and was particularly glad of this opportunity to examine, in a special and practical form, the condition of things inside. The work on that Committee made me acquainted with details which I could scarcely have got to know in any other way, and my recollection of it enables me to tell some of the points of a story which at the time attracted much attention, but which is now, I presume, almost forgotten.

Our Committee had nothing to do with the transport of the stores to Paris; its function was limited to their distribution when they got there. I knew, therefore, nothing, except in a very general way, about the difficulties of carriage and the labour of surmounting them; I remember only that great energy was employed, that much credit was due to those who had charge of the forwarding from the ports, and that Colonel Wortley and Mr Moore were indefatigable. Their first act was to organise depots all over the town, especially in the poorer districts. I forget how many there were, but I am under the impression that the number was between a dozen and twenty. There were, frequently, delays in conveying the stores from the railway station to the depots, because of the scarcity of horses; and the unpacking and division into portions for each applicant took up a good deal of time. If we could have given a whole cheese to one, a whole ham to a second, a box of biscuits to a third, and a bag of coffee to a fourth, and have left them to settle the sharing between them, we should have got on much faster; but, as it was, we were often forced to keep the people waiting while hundreds of heaps of varied provisions, in a transportable condition, were prepared in rows. When once that was done, the handing out went on very fast. At each depot a staff was installed, and, during the earlier days, the task of giving went on uninterruptedly, even at night. Paris knew within twenty-four hours that food was to be had for the asking, and Paris came in crowds to ask for it. The crowds, in themselves, supplied no reliable testimony of the existence of great want, for they would appear again to-day, in equal numbers, if food were once more offered for nothing; but in their aspect and their composition there were details which showed, in some degree at least, that the nature of the occasion was special. Again, the food was, of necessity, distributed haphazard, and the process in itself revealed little on the surface; but on the rare occasions when it was possible to penetrate into it, to learn the secrets of the starvelings, and to discover the personal causes which led them to come and beg, it assumed a totally different character, and became at moments intensely interesting.

For many days I passed a considerable portion of my time in the depots, or outside them talking to the waiting mob, and I heard a quantity of tales of suffering, the majority of which were, I fancy (judging from the manner of telling, or from the nature of the statements), mainly imaginary, while some few of them were, I daresay, painfully true. I repeat, however, before narrating stories, that I regarded the authentic ones as exceptions, and that the famine provoked by the siege alone, and not by general or accidental causes, was not so serious as the European public had supposed. Other witnesses may, possibly, hold a precisely contrary opinion: I speak solely for myself, after a careful study of the situation, so far as I could measure it, and after diligent inquiry amongst those who were best placed to know the facts.

The first depot opened was somewhere near the Church of Notre Dame des Victoires; and, as it was the first, the rush to it was great. The column of people was indeed so long that it stretched, six or eight thick, almost a quarter of a mile away, past the Bourse. Several of us went down on the first evening and found men and women standing or sitting on the pavements, a few with wraps, many without. Various classes were represented amongst them: some looked not only respectable, but almost as if they belonged to the lower middle strata; the vast majority, however, were the poorest of the poor, and seemed wretchedly unfit, with their tattered clothes, to support twelve or fifteen hours of waiting in the bitter air. It was so dark (there was no gas, for the reason that there was no coal to make it with) that we could

not see clearly; but our eyes had grown somewhat accustomed to the gloom, and we were
able, on looking closely, to perceive approximately the features of the people, and sometimes the expressions of their faces. As we
peered into the thicknesses of the crowd and
sought for revelations of the nature of its
elements, a lady with us—Madame de V.—
happened to notice a woman leaning wearily
against a lamp-post. She spoke to her, and
was told one of the usual stories of children
starving, a drunken husband, no fire, and no
food; and as she looked nearer still, she became
aware that the woman was far advanced in
pregnancy, seemed miserably weak, and was
assuredly in no condition to pass a night on
the icy stones. So, after exchanging a few
words with Colonel Wortley, Madame de V.
said to the woman in a low voice, in order that
the others might not hear, "I know the English
people who are distributing the food, and as
you are so unfit to await your turn, I have
obtained permission from them to go into the
depot and to bring you out some provisions.
Wait at this lamp-post till I come back."
Then, after taking a few steps towards the
depot, it occurred to Madame de V. that she

had nothing in which to carry loaves and meat; so she went back to the woman and whispered to her, "Give me your apron to bring it in." At this proposal the woman shrank back suspiciously, thinking evidently that it was a mere trick to steal her apron; whereon Madame de V. went on, with ready thought, "And as I shall need both my hands to hold the corners of the apron, I will ask you to be so kind as to keep my muff for me while I am gone."   This pacified the woman, for she had sense enough to recognise that a sable muff was worth more than a blue apron; so she untied the strings, muttering, "Well, I hope it's all right; but don't be long."   Ten minutes afterwards Madame de V. was back again with as heavy a weight as her arms could carry, and then a new difficulty arose. The woman in her eagerness almost flung the muff at its owner, seized the bundle feverishly, did not stop to thank, and hurried off; but the neighbours in the crowd, observing what had happened, claimed noisily, almost brutally, the same privilege, declaring that it was a shame to do for one what was not done for all, and asserting that the woman had no rights superior to theirs.   As they began to grow threatening, and as there were no police, two or three of us stood in between them and Madame de V., while others got her away, pursued by abuse, into the shelter of the depot. The incident was not pleasant, but it gave us the measure of some of the characters we had to deal with, and it supplied new evidence in support of the theory (which is so widely held) that it is folly to be kind.

Inside the depot the sight was curious. It was our first experience, and we all looked on intently. The people came in, singly, through one door, and passed out at another; and, as each man or woman advanced suddenly into the light, the astonishing variety of their expressions struck us all. Many looked so brokenly fagged that their faces had lost all other meaning; others, on the contrary, had become uncontrollably excited; some were savage with ill-temper, and some trembling with joy; some were sullen, and some were eager; the eyes of some stared at us scowlingly and defiantly; the eyes of others brightened gluttonously as they caught sight of the piles of biscuits, cheeses, and hams, and the packets of coffee and sugar; some (a very small minority) thanked enthusiastically, with tears in their eyes; others grasped almost fiercely the objects handed to them, and rushed out into the darkness to begin munching. On the whole, it was a distressing sight, and I imagine that we all went to bed that night with an uncomfortable sensation in our throats.

On other occasions, in the daytime, I was able to look with more scrutiny and more fruit at the composition of the waiting crowd, and my general impression was that it was more miserable, more ill-conditioned, and, especially, more evil-faced, than even the dirtiest crowds usually are. A good many persons in it were relatively decent; honesty and goodness—mixed with anxiety and fatigue—could be perceived in the features of several of its members; but the general effect produced by it was one of extreme wretchedness; and, worse than all, it contained, here and there, some of those strangely awful faces — the faces of habitual criminals — which, when perceived suddenly, almost choke those who catch sight of them. In some Paris prisons, and in all Paris street-fightings, I had beheld, with bewilderment and horror, an infamy of expression in many coun-tenances which exceeded all that imagination usually conceives. In the ordinary conditions of life such faces are never to be found in Paris;

it is only in jails and during revolutions that they can be seen in any numbers; and it was behind bars or barricades that I had perceived them so far. Yet there they were in the street, physiognomies so appallingly depraved, so be-fouled with degradations and defilements, so denaturalised by hideous appetites, that gorillas would have seemed angels of purity beside them, — physiognomies that, without actually staring at them, no one could have supposed possible in man. They could not be described as animal, for no animal is capable of expressing such pollution or of exhibiting such vice; they had a meaning which humanity alone, dragged down to its deepest corruption, can convey. Well, in the crowds awaiting food those faces were rather frequently represented: I saw them there in the open air for the first time—except during a revolution. Of course, they were not really abundant; but the excessiveness of their horror, so infinitely more out of place in the brightness of sunlight than in the darkness of prison or amidst the violence of a riot, seemed to multiply them, until, in a waking nightmare, I saw them everywhere. There they were, in liberty and peace, conditions which, till then, I had never associated with them; and they showed no shame. Their right to the "English gifts" was as real as that of all the others; and yet the others, even the most wretched of them, shrank instinctively away from them, and left around them a ring of empty space. But the creatures with those faces did not perceive their solitude,—they did not even seek to collect together and support each other: each one of them stood apart, alone; from each of them seemed to exude a separate and distinct atmosphere of abomination. As I watched them, a friend whispered to me, " Where do those gentlemen live when they are at home? I should like to know, so as not to call on them."

The spectacle of the weary column was so saddening that it did not need the additional impress of the presence of those monsters. Yet there they were, and there was no disputing their title to be there. The food was for anybody who chose to ask for it: they asked. It will be a comparative relief to my memory to begin talking again about the depots.

Yet the scenes in them were neither varied nor agreeable; they were, indeed, both monotonous and disagreeable, and, after the first effect upon us had worn off, we looked on at them with weariness of spirit. It did not suffice to keep up our attention to tell ourselves that the men were French electors, and therefore politically our equals; that the women were wives and mothers (or, at all events, daughters), and our fellow-beings; and that all of them deserved our sympathy because they were hungry: we did not, when a day or two had passed, find those considerations effective. We discovered we were there to discharge a duty, not to satisfy a curiosity, and the duty became ugly. Never did I perceive so clearly the value of curiosity as a stimulant and encouragement. As it faded away, that mob, which, at the beginning, had seemed to me so full of the promise of interesting discoveries, assumed more and more its proper aspect of dirty misery and uninstructive repulsiveness: it told me nothing, and it smelt very nasty. And I could not disguise from myself that it lowered my idea of humanity, and that it became unpleasant to me to recognise that, after all, I was identical with those repellent persons, and was differentiated from them solely by the accident that I had received an education and they had not. Fortunately I had not much time to indulge my disagreeable sensations; but I mention them because they formed part of the day's work, and because they showed that some. training is needed (in many cases, at all events) to fit us to endure contact with filth and unwholesomeness. Those processions through the depots were distinctly trying, and, with individual exceptions, distinctly tiresome. Now that I have sufficiently described their main features, I can turn away from them, and can begin to talk of the more attractive subject of individual exceptions.

One of the most important of these depots was installed in the then unfinished shop of the Bon Marché, which had been built just before the war broke out. The proprietor of the establishment—M. Aristide Boucicaut, who was an excellent man, as well as a prodigious linen-draper—had offered the use of his great ground-floor, with a special entrance at the angle opposite the end of the Rue de Sèvres, where there was a large open *place*. As the neighbourhood was poor and populous, a considerable supply of food was accumulated there, in anticipation of a large crowd, and public notice was given of the moment at which the distribution would commence. More than twenty-four hours before the hour named

people began to collect at the corner, and
when the morning came the entire space was
filled with a restless crowd, the greater part
of which had passed the night there. There
must have been ten thousand persons assembled,
two-thirds of whom were women. About eleven
o'clock the members of the Committee reached
the Bon Marché, and were joined by several
friends. The first news given to us was that
the impatience of the mob was growing dangerous, and, especially, that the pressure at the
corner was so violent that, if it could not be
relieved, there would inevitably be accidents.
Unfortunately, the preparations for distribution
were not complete: another hour was needed
before a sufficient number of portions could be
got ready, and the question was how to hold
the people steady in the interval. Some of
us went to the window on the first floor and
looked out. It was an ugly and a painful
sight. The instant we appeared, thousands of
white faces, some furious, some beseeching,
turned up to us, and cries arose that we were
deceiving them, that the hour was past, and
that they ought to be let in. Screams of
terrified, half-stifled women rang through the
air, as the mob swayed and surged. There

were half a dozen of us at that window, staring at the sight, but the only two that I remember were Laurence Oliphant and Mr Lan-
dells, the artist of the 'Illustrated London
News': there were two or three of the Embassy as well, but I forget which of them. We
shouted to the people, entreating them to
stand still, and promising that the door should
be opened the instant we were ready; but
they could not hear for the noise they were
making, and we grew more and more certain
that some of them would be crushed if we could
find no means of making them stand back.
While we were hesitating what to do, we saw
that a woman had fallen beneath the window
and was being trampled on. Thereon we all
ran anxiously down-stairs; M. Boucicaut managed to force open the upper half of the iron
shutter of the ground-floor corner window, and
he and I scrambled on to the top of some
empty cases, so as to be able to look out above
the mob and try to save the woman. Directly
we put our heads out, some eight feet from
the ground, we beheld just under us, between
the people, portions of what looked like a
bundle of rags mixed with arms and legs, the
others stamping on it from sheer impossibility

of resisting the thrust from behind. It was sickening to see the poor creature killed under our eyes in that way, and we roared out supplications to the mob to spare her and to hold back, if only for an instant, while she was lifted out. In some strange way, by a fierce effort of the front ranks, there came two seconds of recoil; three other women got space enough to stoop and to pick up the lamentable bundle, and, stretching out our arms till we nearly fell out of the window ourselves, we managed to get hold of it and to bring it up to our level, the nearer portions of the crowd cheering as we got it in. A moment later we were on the floor with our burden, and laid it on a counter. It was a youngish woman, white, insensible, bleeding from small cuts, covered with dirt, her clothes in pieces. We bathed her face and hands, and, after a while, got her round, so far at least that she could begin to speak a little. At first she was only dimly conscious, and very breathless, and seemed bewildered with terror; but by degrees she became calm, gained a little strength, and told us she had passed thirty hours standing at that corner, had felt the pressure gradually increasing, and, suddenly, had known no more. We gave her cold beef-tea (the only liquid food we had), with bread soaked in it, and, as soon as she was able to stand, got up a little subscription for her amongst ourselves, filled a basket with various food, and when, after an hour of rest, she had grown comparatively strong, sent her on her way by another door.

By the time she was gone everything was at last ready, and the door was opened. The first rush rather overpowered us: the pushing was violent; the weaker were thrown down; but, on the whole, the people behaved well, and waited for their turn without too much complaint.

And now I am going to tell the story of the woman we dragged in, for the reason that it supplies an example of a really bad case brought about by the siege alone, and shows exactly what was the nature and the course of the siege distress, when that distress was real. I felt, instinctively, a sort of personal responsibility about that woman, and had a vague impression that, as I had helped somewhat to save her life, I ought not to stop there, but was bound to go on and to try to discover what her needs were, and whether anything practical could be done for her.   I had asked for her address, privately, when nobody was near, and next morning, without telling any one of my intention, I went to her. On my way I was oppressed by a peculiar sensation of awkwardness, almost indeed of shame, such as is experienced, I have been told, by most people when they attempt for the first time to perform "good works." I certainly had never done a "good work" in my life, and I well remember how nervously I hoped that nobody would suspect me, and that I should not be found out. I can talk about it tranquilly now, but at the time I felt like a culprit on the point of being arrested. The woman lived in the Rue St Jacques, on a fifth floor, in a poor but decent house. When I got up to her door my feeling of timidity and clumsiness increased. I felt stupidly bashful, reproached myself for coming at all, and was strongly tempted to go away. I recollect that I found consolation solely in the fact that no one met me on the stairs. I stared for a moment at the bell (I can see it still: it was a little brass chain, with a chamois-foot hanging at the end), and, finally, rang it with a somewhat convulsive effort. The situation was so new to me that all the details are impressed on my memory. No one came, but I heard a faint cry of "Entrez," and I opened the door. In a large but almost empty room my acquaintance of the day before was lying. on a bed. She blushed violently, rose hastily, and began to excuse herself, saying that she had supposed it was the *concierge*. She was evidently extremely uncomfortable, but I cannot believe that she was half so uneasy as I was. I had prepared a speech, but it faded out of my head, and all I could do was to beg her to forgive me for coming, and to pretend that I wanted to know how she was; and then, abruptly—rather roughly, I fear—I asked her to tell me the details of her life during the siege. She seemed surprised at my request, and un-willing to comply with it; but by degrees, in a disorderly fashion, she did confess what I wanted to know. Here is the substance of the story I got out of her.

She had been an artificial - flower - maker, with abundant occupation. She had indeed developed such a particular capacity for the manufacture of tea-roses, that she had obtained for the two preceding years almost the exclusive supply of three of the large shops, employed two girls to help her, and earned the high average profit of ten francs a-day. Being a thrifty woman, she laid by money, and had bought four debentures of the Northern Railway, which brought her in an income of more than two guineas a-year—"a beginning of a fortune," as she observed, with a faint smile. When the war broke out she did not realise its meaning; she supposed it would be over in a few weeks, and, as she had two hundred francs in a corner of a drawer, felt quite safe about money, even if her work remained stopped for a while. But prices went up so fast and so high that the two hundred francs were gone in a month. Then she began to sell the railway debentures at a great loss, and this product disappeared also very quickly. So by the end of the second month she had to turn her clothes and furniture into such cash as they would fetch, and at last, in December, she found herself entirely destitute, with scarcely anything left except her bed and the gown and shawl she wore. Happily, as the payment of rent had been suspended by the Government at the commencement of the siege, the landlord could not turn her out for default, and she was able for the moment to remain in her room. Then came the worst part of all—the waiting, for hours a day in bitter cold, at the baker's door for her pittance of black tallowy bread that made her ill. A cough began; she grew weak; and when at last the investment was over, she was exhausted in body, in mind, and in purse, and was, furthermore, haunted by the terror that in a short time the protection about rent would come to an end, that her arrears would be due, and that she would be turned into the street. Then she heard that food (not the nastiness of the siege, but real white bread!) was going to be given away for nothing at the Bon Marché, and she was one of the first to take a place at that corner door.

She told me all this very disjointedly, with a great deal of hesitation and of evident dislike to talk about herself to a stranger, but with an air of truth that convinced me. I learnt from her also that she was known to one of the curates of the parish of St Jacques du Haut Pas, so, on leaving her, I went straight to him and asked him what he could tell me about her. He happened to be a very noble specimen of a priest, full of practical common-sense, and of infinite experience of the forms of pain. He informed me that he had been acquainted with the woman for some years, and that her story was perfectly exact so far as it went, but that there was a good deal more behind. First, that

she had a drag upon her in the shape of a
paralysed old aunt, who was finishing her days
somewhere in Auvergne, and to whom she had
paid a pension of a franc a-day. Secondly, that,
although she managed to lay by money, she
had always some to give to those who were
poorer than herself, and that, during the siege,
she had shared her savings and the product of
her sales with any one who needed help. Third-
ly, that her health had become so weakened,
and the moral impression on her of the events
that had passed around her had been so damaging, that he feared she would have great
difficulty in recovering strength, and that he
was trying to get money from charitable persons
in order to send her (and others) to the seaside,
for change and rest.

He gave me also a good deal of detail about
the sufferings of which he had been a spectator
during the siege, and added strength to the impression I had already begun to form, that there
had been no general starvation. He told me, of
course, of many people who were, more or less,
in want, and asked me to take a list of women
to whom food could be supplied privately, with
the certainty that it was both needed and deserved; and then, when I begged to be allowed

to contribute my mite to the necessities around him, refused to accept anything from me, saying that the English had done quite enough in organising the food gifts.

By the time our conversation came to an end, I had pretty nearly got over my sheepishness, and was beginning, with the sudden ardour of a neophyte, to be immensely interested in "good works," which, like many others, I had regarded until then from the top of my indifference. So, in my new enthusiasm, I went back to the Hôtel Chatham, told Oliphant in secrecy the story of my morning's work, and consulted him as to what we should do about the woman. We devised a beautifully constructed little plan, quite within our small powers of realisation, and of the invention of which we felt very proud; but, alas! we were unable to carry it into execution. The poor creature became too ill to leave Paris; she dragged on through the Commune, and died of exhaustion in July. At all events her latter days were calm, and not poisoned by money worries. We two, with a group of her own friends and that good priest, saw the last of her in the Montparnasse Cemetery. Often did Oliphant and I talk together of her afterwards, for we remembered her as a patient, brave, good woman. Yet neither of us ever told her story: somehow we both shrank from speaking of it to others. Now, however, that a quarter of a century has passed, I think I may venture, with deep respect for the memory of the poor flower-maker, to put the tale in here, because, as I have already said, it supplies a reliable illustration of the worst consequences of the siege.

The experience of a few days, and the rapid multiplication of the demands for private assistance, irrespective of the public distributions at the depots, decided Colonel Wortley and the committee to open a special store for the issue of provisions by ticket, so as to free the better class of poor from the strain and shame of waiting in the streets. A convenient place was obtained for the purpose in a quiet corner near the Boulevard Malesherbes, and I suspect that much more real good was done there, and more true suffering soothed, than by all the indiscriminate public givings. It was, of course, extremely difficult to obtain information about the people who went there, for in most cases the tickets were placed by other persons, and we had no more means of following out the work we were doing than in the ordinary universal distributions; but I was able occasionally to lift up a corner of the veil, and to get a glimpse of what was passing underneath.

Most of the cases of this category about which I managed to collect information were of the ordinary kind, and are not worth describing: clerks and *employés* of all sorts, and high-class workmen and workwomen, had found their pay stopped, had exhausted their slender resources, and had struggled with the usual difficulties. In a few instances, however, the circumstances were special and grave, only I was rarely able to learn the whole truth, so as to have an entire story before me, and can therefore say nothing interesting about the majority of them. So far as I can recollect, there were but two of which, by accident, I heard full details, and which were sufficiently outside the ordinary types of distress for it to be worth while to tell them here.

The first concerned a retired artillery officer, with a wife, a son, and a daughter, who lived together in a little apartment near the Place de l'Europe. Until the war came they got on fairly well: they were very poor, but they managed to subsist without running into debt; the father gave lessons in mathematics, the son was clerk in a bank, the daughter taught the piano. The siege stopped their various incomes: the father's little pension continued, perhaps, to be paid to him, but of that I am not certain; all the rest disappeared. The father, old and feeble as he was, offered his services on the ramparts; but on the second day, in getting a gun into an embrasure, his leg was broken in two places, and he was carried to a hospital, where he remained until the capitulation. The son became a National Guard, and rarely showed himself to his mother and sister, who, from the very beginning of the investment, found themselves alone. In their case, as in so many others, it was on the women that the burden fell. The daughter got into an ambulance as nurse; but she was a weakly creature, of little courage, with susceptible nerves, and when some wounded men were brought in after the first skirmish, she had a hysterical attack, and was turned out by the doctors. The mother, who also was a weak woman, became utterly upset by her misfortunes, reproached the daughter with her uselessness, and a quarrel ensued, whereon the daughter ran out and threw herself into the Seine. At this point of the tale my information became incomplete, and I did not learn how the girl was saved; but saved she was, and was taken in somewhere by some one : so her mother, hearing no more of her, and believing her to be dead, lost the little reason she had, and was put into a lunatic asylum. A few weeks later the daughter re-appeared at her home, found it empty, and was told her mother was insane. Thereon she too grew demented, and, returning to the river, drowned herself for good. Soon afterwards the son disappeared, and it was never known what became of him. So, when the father came out of hospital, at the beginning of February, he found his wife mad, his daughter dead, and his son missing. The poor man's sorrow was terrible, and as he had no means of subsistence, his material distress also was extreme. Happily, when he was absolutely without food, his case became known to some one who was in communication with the English committee; tickets were obtained for him, and so long as the distribution continued (that is to say, till about the end of February, I think), he received a daily allowance. I heard the story from one of the men employed at the private depot, and he informed me some months later that the poor man had been removed into the country by kind people, and that he was to live on his pension, such as it was. But he was alone; his home and family were gone. Decidedly the siege had been hard upon him.

In the second case a designer in a manufactory of bronze figures, a man who counted rather as an artist than an artisan, and who earned easily from seventy to a hundred francs a-week (but who had lived largely and had laid by nothing), lost his eyes six months before the war, by an accident in casting a statue, and became incapable of earning his bread. His wife was dead, but he had two sons and a daughter, all good workers and doing well, and they undertook to pay him, between them, an allowance of three francs a-day until he could be got into the Blind Asylum. When the siege came on, the sons entered the National Guard, and one of them was killed—though seemingly out of range—by a lost bullet in the first skirmish. As the other son had no longer any income other than his pay as a temporary soldier, and as the daughter—who, being tall and slight, had been a lay-figure for the exhibition of mantles and fashions in the rooms of one of the great dressmakers—had of course lost her place by the closing of the establishment, the father and daughter were left, from September, without means of subsistence. For a time, nevertheless, they managed to exist : their former employers gave them small sums ; other people helped them somewhat ; and during the first few weeks they scraped on. But by the end of October these aids came to an end, and they found themselves face to face with destitution. Furthermore, the daughter fell ill ; and to make the situation still worse, the surviving son, who until then had been a steady fellow, took to drink, like so many others during the siege-time, and instead of being a help, became an additional source of affliction to the two poor people. As none of them had any religion, they had never made acquaintance with the clergy of their parish, and could not apply to them for assistance. At last they were reduced to the humiliation of putting down their names at the Bureau de Bienfaisance at the *mairie* of their *arrondissement*—and those who are acquainted with the pride of most of the skilled workmen of Paris, and with the horror they have of public charity, will know that they must indeed have been in deep distress to have resigned themselves to that step. Between hunger, anxiety, and shame, the daughter (who had been

a very smart, almost elegant young woman, dis-
charging in perfection her function of wearing
clothes so skilfully as to tempt buyers with
them) fell into a condition of nervous prostra-
tion, which, at last, rendered her incapable of
walking. And there they were, the blind father
and the shattered daughter, alone in their two
rooms, from which, happily, as I have already
explained, they could not be turned out while
the siege lasted—waiting for death to put an
end to their distress. About the same time,
the second son, weakened by intoxication, caught
typhoid fever and died. Suddenly, unexpected
aid appeared. A girl, who had been employed
by the same dressmaker as the daughter, had
been sheltered by a fairly rich old lady, to
whom her mother had been maid, and who,
having a generous heart, was looking about for
deserving people to assist. The girl bethought
herself of the " tryer-on," of whose deplorable
situation she was vaguely aware, and went to
look for her. She found her, and told her story
to the old lady, who went at once to see her,
and undertook to provide for her. A period
of relief followed : food, fire, and medicines were
supplied to them, and they began to look with
some hope to the future. But in December the

old lady got a chill, and died in three days; whereon the situation of the father and daughter became even worse than before, because of the fierce cold, against which they could not battle. The other girl (who continued to be cared for by the relatives of the old lady) behaved well, shared with the two the little she had, went to the baker for their bread allowance, and kept them both just alive till the capitulation. Then came the public announcement of the " English gifts," whereon some of my friends, knowing that I was concerned in the distribution, came or wrote to me recommending cases. At first I tried to make some examination for myself, but very soon I was beaten by the accumulation of demands, and, after consulting Colonel Wortley, told my friends they must assume the responsibility of their suggestions, and placed tickets at their disposal. In this way I was asked for help for the father and daughter by a connection, as I discovered afterwards, of the deceased old lady, to whom the other girl had spoken about them. One morning I was in the private-distribution depot looking on, when that very girl came in. I spoke to her, asked whether she was there for herself or for others, and got from her in minute details (rather too minute indeed, for she was an hour over them) the story I have just told. I did not visit the poor people, for by that time I had too much to do, and also was growing a little hardened; but I inquired often about them during two or three years from the friend who had first spoken of them to me, and was pleased to hear that the father was alive, and that the daughter (who was maintaining him) had returned to her place, where she continued to be as elegant as before, and displayed the apparel she was commissioned to put on with a seductively languid new grace, which she was supposed to owe to her sufferings during the siege, and which the others envied. I thought sometimes of going to look at her; but my curiosity seemed to me somewhat indiscreet, and, besides, I fancied that to behold her all over satin and lace might damage the keenness of my sympathy with her sad story.

The case was illustrative. The blindness of the father had nothing to do with the war; but the deaths of the two sons were due to it, one directly, the other indirectly, and the miseries of the daughter were caused by it alone. A better example could scarcely be found of mischief brought about by the siege; yet here again the damage did not assume entirely the shape of starvation—want of food certainly played a part in it, but the deaths of the brothers were not caused by famine, and both the father and daughter lived on and got well.

And there ends my personal knowledge of remarkable sorrows resulting from the investment. I was in a position to look somewhat behind the scenes; I was exceptionally placed, as a member of the English Committee, for hearing of particularly bad examples; I listened to the talk and the experiences of a large number of persons, with many priests amongst them, —and yet I cannot call to mind any other very distressing examples. I heard, of course, in general terms, of many more; but I had no means of testing them, and therefore, though I in no way pretend that there were not hundreds quite as sad as the few I have narrated, I hold nevertheless to the conviction that the siege did not produce anything approaching to the starvation that was gratuitously attributed to it. If evidence could not be found when it was carefully sought for (and I did seek it carefully), it does not seem unjust to infer that it scarcely existed in any abundance. The effect of the siege was, as I have said and shown, to kindle much disease and much moral and physical distress: its consequences, for years afterwards, showed themselves in many cases of enfeebled health and of damaged constitutions; but those consequences were generated, I believe, by cold, by anxiety, by gloomy surroundings, and by unwholesome nourishment, far more than by positive absence of any food whatever. If the siege had occurred in the summer, instead of the winter, the larger part of those consequences would not, in all probability, have come about at all.

I am therefore disposed to doubt whether the "English gifts" did all the good that was intended and expected by their promoters. That they did some good is certain; that they enabled a good many people to make the first fair meal they had eaten for a long while, is equally certain; that, here and there, in a few cases, they supplied food just at the last moment, when it seemed to be unobtainable elsewhere, is, I think, proved by the stories I have told; but as there was no general absolute starvation, their influence went no further. It was a satisfaction to every one concerned to feel that those results were attained; but the hope was to do much more, and more was not done, for the decisive reason that it was not there to do.

Furthermore, though it pleased the English to send the food, I doubt strongly that it pleased the French to receive it. The circumstances were delicate: the French were at that moment, most naturally, in a condition of nerve-tension, of rage, of humiliation, which led them to look at everything with a fiercely embittered eye; and a good many of them imagined, in their rankling susceptibility, that the object of England was to humiliate them rather than to assist them. And, honestly, considering what their state of mind was at the time; considering that they were writhing under defeat and pain; considering how unprepared they had been, both by their national character and by the previous conditions of their national life, to stand up under the fearful blow that fell upon them,—I admit that they had much excuse for their impression. The question was not whether the impression itself was true or false, but whether those who formed it were led to it by what appeared to them, in their excitement, to be a reasonable feeling. Their irritation was such that, in many cases, it was almost unsafe for a foreigner to speak to them. That irritation

was, if not justifiable, at all events compre-
hensible, and it influenced every thought they
had. Even long afterwards I heard the "English gifts" referred to with resentment. The
Government of the period professed, officially,
to be very grateful, and to be much touched
by the sympathy exhibited by England; and
of course the people who got the food were
glad to profit by it: but I am convinced that
the nation, as a whole, disliked our interference,
and would have preferred to see us "stop in
our island."

CHAPTER VI.

In the early morning of 1st March 1871, Laurence Oliphant (who was then correspondent of the 'Times') and I left the Hôtel Chatham to walk up the Champs Elysées to a balcony in the Avenue de la Grande Armée, from which we were to view the entry of the Germans into Paris. The sky was grey; the air was full of mist; not a soul was to be seen; the shutters of every house were closed; a day of national humiliation could not have commenced more dismally. I remember that we felt an oppressive sensation of loneliness and gloom, which we communicated to each other at the same instant, and then laughed at the simultaneity of our thoughts.

At the Arch of Triumph were two men in blouses, the first we met. They were staring through the mist at the Porte Maillot, and we proceeded to stare too, for it was from that gate that the entry was to be made. So far as we could see, the whole place was absolutely empty; but our eyes were not quite reliable, for the fog on the low ground was so thick that it was impossible to make out anything. That fog might be full of troops, for all we knew.

It was then about half-past seven, and as we had been told the night before that the advanced-guard would come in at eight, we thought, after standing for some minutes on the heaps of gravel which had been thrown up during the siege to form a trench and barricade under and around the Arch, that we had better move on to our balcony. Meanwhile, however, some twenty or thirty other blouses, evil-faced and wretched, had come up; they eyed us with undisguised suspicion, and consulted each other, apparently, as to what we could be, and what they should do to us. We left them hesitating, and walked on.

A group of Englishmen gathered on that balcony—a dozen curious sight-seers. The owner of the house was Mr Corbett, who was afterwards minister at Stockholm; amongst the others, so far as I remember, were Mr Elliot, the Duke of Manchester, Captain Trotter, and Lord Ronald

Gower. Excepting the men in blouses about the Arch, who by this time had multiplied to at least a hundred, there was nobody within sight. The void was painful. Not a window was open (excepting in the rooms to which we had come); our balcony alone was peopled; one of the greatest historic spectacles of our time was about to be enacted in front of us; yet, save ourselves and the blouses, there was no public to contemplate it. The French who lived up there refused to look, or, if they did look, it was from behind their shutters. Such part of the educated population as were in Paris that day (most of them were absent) hid themselves in grief. We English represented the rest of the world, as we generally do on such occasions.

We gazed hard at the Porte Maillot, from which we were distant about a quarter of a mile; but though the mist had begun to lift a little, it was still too thick to allow anything to be distinguished clearly on the Neuilly road. We looked and looked again in vain. It was not till we had waited, somewhat impatiently, for half an hour, that, at a quarter past eight, some one exclaimed, "I do believe I see moving specks out there beyond the gate." Up went all our glasses, and there they were ! We recognised more and more distinctly six horsemen coming, and evidently coming fast, for they grew bigger and sharper as each second passed. One seemed to be in front, the other five behind.

As we watched eagerly they reached the open gate, dashed through it, and, the instant they were inside, the five behind spread out right and left across the broad avenue, as if to occupy it. The one in front, who, so far as we could see, had been riding until then at a canter, broke into a hand-gallop, and then into a full gallop, and came tearing up the hill. As he neared us we saw he was a hussar officer—a boy—he did not look eighteen! He charged past us, his sword uplifted, his head thrown back, his eyes fixed straight before him, and one of us cried out, " By Jove, if that fellow's mother could see him she'd have something to be proud of for the rest of her time ! " The youngster raced on far ahead of his men, but at the Arch of Triumph the blouses faced him. So, as he would not ride them down in order to go through (and if he had tried it he would only have broken his own neck and his horse's too in the trench), he waved his sword at them, and at slackened speed passed round. We caught sight of him on the other side through the archway, his sword high up, as if he were saluting the vanquished city at his· feet. But he did not stop for sentiment. He cantered on, came back, and as his five men had got up by that time (he had outpaced them by a couple of minutes), he gave them orders, and off they went, one to each diverging avenue, and rode down it a short distance to see that all was right.

The boy trotted slowly round and round the Arch, the blouses glaring at him.

The entry was over—that is to say, the Germans were inside Paris. That boy had done it all alone. The moral effect was produced. Nothing more of that sort could be seen from the balcony. We took it for granted that the rest, when it came, would only be a march past, and that thenceforth the interest of the drama would be in the street. So to the street Oliphant and I returned, two others accompanying us. The remainder of the party, if I remember right, stopped where they were for some time longer.

Just as we got to the Arch the boy came round once more. I went to him and asked his name.

" What for ? " he inquired.

" To publish it in London to - morrow morning."

" Oh! that's it, is it ? " he remarked, with a tinge of the contempt for newspapers which all German officers display. " Well, I'm von Bernhardi, 14th Hussars. Only, if you're going to print it, please give my captain's name also; he's von Colomb."

Five minutes later a squadron of the regiment came up, and Lieutenant von Bernhardi's command-in-chief expired. But the youngster had made a history for his name; he was the first German into Paris in 1871.

(I heard, the last time I was in Germany, that the brave boy Bernhardi is dead, and that Colomb was then colonel of the King's Hussars, at Bonn.)

We stood amongst the blouses, and wondered whether they would wring our necks. We were clean, presumably we had money in our pockets, and I had spoken to a German—three unpardonable offences. No attack, however, was made on any of us for the moment. Now that I look back on the particular circumstances, I fail to comprehend why they were good enough to abstain.

More and more troops marched up, infantry

and cavalry, but always in small numbers; the mass of the German army was at Longchamp, for the great review to be held that morning by the Emperor, and the 30,000 men who, under the convention of occupation, were to enter Paris (in reality, about 40,000 came), were not to appear till the review was over.

At nine o'clock the commander of the occupation (General von Kameke) rode in with an escort. At his side was Count Waldersee, who during the war had been chief of the staff to the Duke of Mecklenburg, to whose army Oliphant had been attached. Seeing Waldersee, Oliphant jumped out to greet him, shook hands with him warmly, chatted gaily, and, after showing various signs of intimacy, came back towards us laughing, as the other rode on. This was, not unnaturally, too much for those of the blouses who saw it, and, before Oliphant could reach us, they rushed at him. Some hit him, some tried to trip him up; a good dozen of them were on him. A couple of us made a plunge after him, roared to the blouses that he was an Englishman, and that they had no right to touch him; and somehow (I have never understood how) we pulled him out undamaged, but a good deal out of breath and with his jacket torn.

The blouses howled at us, and bestowed un-gentle epithets on us, and followed us, and men-aced; but we got away into another part of the constantly thickening crowd, and promised each other that we would speak no more that day to Germans. I need scarcely say that the mob was unchecked master, that the Germans would not have interfered in any fight that did not directly concern them, and that neither a French policeman nor a French soldier was present to keep order within the limits of the district fixed for the occupation. Those limits were — the Place de la Concorde on the east, the Faubourg St. Honoré and the Avenue des Ternes on the north, the Seine on the south.

By ten the sun had worked through the fog, and also, by ten, a considerable number of the inhabitants of Paris had become unable to resist the temptation of seeing a new sight, and had come out to the show. At that hour there must have been 30,000 or 40,000 people in the upper part of the Champs Elysées; the gloom of the early morning was as if it had not been; all was movement and brightness. The crowd, which in the afternoon we estimated at 100,000 to 150,000, was composed, for the greater part, of blouses; but mixed with them were a quantity of decent people, from all parts of the town, women and children as well as men, belonging, apparently, to the classes of small shopkeepers, employees, and workmen. From morning to night I did not perceive one single gentleman (excepting a foreigner here and there); nor was a shutter opened in the Champs Elysées. The upper strata kept out of sight; it was the other *couches*, especially the very lowest, that had come out.

Directly troops enough were in to supply pickets, sentries were posted at the street-corners; patrols were set going; a guard was mounted at the house of Queen Christina, in the Champs Elysées, which had been selected for the German headquarters. We looked on at all this, at first with close attention, but by degrees the state of things grew rather dull. In times of great excitement, events seem to become stupid so soon as they cease, temporarily, to be dangerous. Besides, for the moment, the interest of the day had changed its place and nature; it was no longer in the German army, but in the French crowd; not in the entry, but in the reception. As we had rightly judged, the drama was in the street. So we stood about and watched the people, and talked to some of them, and thought that, on the whole, they behaved very well. Of course they would have done better still if they had stopped at home, and had left the Germans severely alone; but, as they had thought fit to come, they also thought fit to keep their tempers, which was creditable to them. So long as they were not provoked by some particular cause, they remained quiet and showed no rage. They wanted to behold a remarkable sight that was offered for their inspection, and though beyond doubt it vexed them, their vexation was not strong enough to check their curiosity. At least that was our impression from what we saw.

At half-past one I had wandered back alone to the Avenue de la Grande Armée, where the crowd had become very dense, filling up, indeed, the entire roadway. On the other side I saw a horseman trying to work his way through. It was Mr W. H. Russell. I could not get to him to speak, but I knew by his presence there that the review (to which he had ridden from Versailles) was over, and that, before very long, the real march in would commence. It did not occur to me at the moment that Mr Russell was doing a risky thing in cutting across the mob on a prosperous horse, which manifestly had not gone through the siege-time in Paris. It was not till some hours later that I learnt how nearly the mob had killed him.

At last, at two o'clock, thick dust arose outside the Porte Maillot, and I made out with my glass that the people were being pressed back at the gate, and that troops were advancing slowly—for the mob would not make way, and the Germans were patient and gentle with them. The head of the column got up creepingly as far as the Arch of Triumph; but then came a dead block. The gathering of people filled up the Place de l'Etoile and the upper part of the Avenue des Champs Elysées, and packed it all so solidly that often, for minutes at a time, the cavalry could not move ahead. A good half-hour passed before space was cleared for the staff; and even then, for nearly another half-hour after they had reached the Neuilly side of the Arch, they had to sit still upon their horses, unable to progress one yard.

And what a staff it was! With the exception of the Crown Prince Frederick, every prince in the army—and that meant almost every prince in Germany—and heaps of officers of high rank, had come up from the review to take part in the ride in. At their head, alone, sat the late

Duke Ernest of Saxe-Coburg, taking precedence as the senior reigning sovereign present. Behind him were rows on rows of members of the royal and historic families of Germany, some twenty in a row, and, including aides-de-camp and orderlies, some thirty rows! In every sort and colour of uniform, they stretched across the full width of the great Avenue from curbstone to curbstone, and would have filled up the pathways too if they had not been already choked with French spectators. I had the good fortune to penetrate to the corner of the pavement where the Place de l'Etoile opens out, and there I stood and gazed.

The sun shone splendidly; the mob stared silently; the princes waited tranquilly.

I recognised many faces that I had got to know at Versailles during the siege. I saw Meiningens, and Leopold Hohenzollern, and Altenburgs, and Lippes, and Reuss, and Pless, and Schœnburgs, Waldecks, Wieds, Hohenlohes, and Mecklenburgs, and the bearers of other names that are written large in the chronicles of the Fatherland.

And as I went on looking, my eyes fell on to the front rank, and the fourth man in that rank was—Bismarck.

His right hand was twisted into his horse's mane; his helmeted head hung down upon his chest, so low that I could perceive nothing of his face except the tip of his nose and the ends of his moustache. There he sat, motionless, evidently in deep thought. After I had watched him for a couple of minutes (I need scarcely say that, having discovered him, I ceased to look at anybody else), he raised his head slowly and fixed his eyes on the top of the Arch, which was just in front of him, some eighty yards off. In that position he remained, once more motionless, for a while. I did my best—he was only the thickness of three horses from me—to make out the expression of his face, which was then fully exposed to me; but there was no marked expression on it. At that moment of intense victory, when all was won, inside surrendered Paris, with the whole world thinking of him, he seemed indifferent, fatigued, almost sad.

Suddenly I saw that his horse's head was moving from the line; he was coming out. He turned to the right, in my direction; he raised his hand to the salute as he passed before his neighbours to the end of the rank, came straight towards me, and guided his horse in between the column of officers and the tightly jammed crowd on the pavement. It seemed impossible he could find room to pass, so little space was there; but pass he did. The top of his jackboot brushed hard against my waistcoat; but with all my desire to get out of his way I could not struggle backwards, because of the denseness of the throng behind me. No Frenchman recognised him. I have wondered since what would have happened if I had told the people who he was. Would they have gaped at him in hating silence? Would they have cursed him aloud? Would they have flung stones at him? Or would they, as a safer solution, have battered me for the crime of knowing him by sight? He rode on slowly down the hill, making his way with difficulty. I heard next day that, once outside the gate, he trotted straight back to Versailles.

So, on that marvellous occasion—an occasion which he, of all men, had most contributed to create—he did not enter Paris after all (beyond the Arch of Triumph, I mean). A friend to whom I told this story some years later, took an opportunity to ask him what was his reason for riding away and for taking no further part in the day's work. He answered, " Why, I saw that all was going on well, and that there would be no row: I had a lot to do at Versailles, so I went and did it." If that was in reality his sole motive, he proved that he possessed, at that period of his life, a power of self-control which he has lost since; for it must have cost him a good deal to forego the splendid satisfaction of consummating his work by heading the triumphal progress down the Champs Elysées.

At the moment when this happened I was separated from Oliphant; but as we had fixed upon a trysting-place close by, I was able to find him soon, and to tell him of the sight I had just witnessed. He was sorry he had not seen it too, for he was curious about the mental ways of Count Bismarck (as he was then).

At last the cavalry in front succeeded in opening out a way. But what a way! It was a twisting narrow path, all zigzags, curves, and bends; not twenty yards of it were straight. The French stood doggedly; they would not move. With infinite patience, avoiding all brutality, excepting here and there when some soldier lost his temper for a moment and used the flat of his sword, the Germans ended by squeezing the mob just enough to form a crooked lane a few yards wide, between two walls of people, and down that lane the first part of the solemn entry (the only part I saw) was performed. It was not an effective spectacle, nor did the German army, otherwise than by their mere presence there, represent a conquering host; they were vastly too polite for victors, and vastly too irregular for a phalanx. Regarded either as a military pageant or as a blaze of triumph, the entry was a failure. Decidedly young Bernhardi had the best of it. There was sore talking afterwards, amongst the troops that had not come in, about the sacrifice of the glory of Germany to fanciful ideas of respect for the vanquished.

The march down the Champs Élysées commenced about three o'clock, but we did not care to follow it; it was difficult to see anything at all, so wedged in was the column; and, furthermore, we had eaten nothing for nine hours and were desperately hungry. So, as some one told us that a *café* was open at the corner of the Avenue de l'Alma, we went off to it, in hopes. Most happily the report was true; only the place was so crammed with devouring Germans that we could obtain scarcely anything. To punish the owner for feeding the foe, the blouses had the kindness to pull that *café* to pieces two days afterwards, at the moment of the evacuation.

And then we strolled again, and stood about, and listened to the talk of the mob, and noticed more and more that, though full of a dull hate against the enemy, the hate was in no way violent. Curiosity, as I have already said, was more vigorous than rage. Sometimes a blouse would curse an officer, or sneer at one, or even lift a threatening hand (though that was rare); but, on the whole, they were very quiet, and they all ran for their lives if, here and there, a too aggressively provoked German made pretence to ride at them or to raise his sword. I cannot sufficiently repeat that, taking into account the realities of the position, the crowd behaved well. There was some laughing, and a good deal of amused comment on the appearance of the Germans; some scoffed at them, especially at the few who wore the Frederick the Great mitre shakos of the Foot Guards; but some again frankly praised the height and size, and particularly the aristocratic bearing, of many of the officers. A woman at my side gave vent simultaneously to her artistic appreciation of them, and to her indignation at being forced involuntarily to admire them, by exclaiming, " C'est dégoûtant comme ils sont distingués ! "

It was only on the fringes of the crowd, so far as I saw and heard, that attacks were made and cruelties committed, and even there, only against persons who spoke to Germans, or were suspected of being " spies," whatever that might mean. (At that time, the exclamation " Nous sommes trahis " was considered to explain and excuse everything.)   A friend of mine saw a young woman, smartly dressed, but pale and seemingly half starved, trying to talk to some officers at the corner of the Rue de Presbourg in the Avenue Joséphine (now the Avenue Marceau).   And then, when she turned away from them, he also saw, to his sickening disgust, a band of blackguards rush at her.   Within half a minute all her clothes were torn from the unhappy creature, and she was cruelly beaten; and there she stood, shrieking, in the sunlight, with nothing left untattered on her but her stays and boots, her bare flesh bleeding everywhere from cuts.   And this was what those ruffians called " patriotism " !   An hour later I was told that another woman, for a similar offence, had been thrown into the Seine; but my informant had not seen it with his own eyes, as in the other case. Of course these atrocities were the work of the filthiest scum of the population.

By five o'clock, when the troops off duty had been dismissed, the door of every house in the Champs Elysées, and in all the streets within the area of occupation, bore chalk-marks indicating the regiment and the number of men to be billeted there ; and there began to be a clearance in the roadway. So, as there was little to see that we had not already seen, Oliphant and I went to the Embassy, passing through the Faubourg on our way, and observing that the limits of the occupation were guarded on each side by German and by French sentries, face to face, and sometimes not a yard apart. We thought that was not pleasant for the French. At the Embassy we found, as well as I remember, the present Sir E. Malet, the present Sir F. Lascelles, Mr Barrington, and Mr Wodehouse. They told us about Mr W. H. Russell, who, after he had passed me in the Avenue de la Grande Armée, had been set upon by the crowd, who tried to drag him from his horse and lynch him. They took him for an isolated German, in plain clothes, and thought the opportunity was excellent. Nevertheless, by pluck and luck, he had managed to gallop on to the shelter of the Embassy, left his horse there, proceeded on foot to the Northern Station, got to London at midnight, by special boat and train, wrote several columns for the morning's 'Times,' went to bed, and next day returned to Paris.

We heard, at the same time, that Mr Archibald Forbes had been knocked over for speaking to a German, and rather hurt, but that he had been rescued by some of the more decent French members of the crowd, and taken, as prisoner, to the nearest Mairie, where he had been released.

After resting for a while, we went back into the Champs Elysées by the Embassy garden-gate in the Avenue Gabriel, so as to avoid the pressure in the Faubourg. We fancied that the French had already grown somewhat accustomed to the presence of the " Prussians," as they called all the Germans indiscriminately. It was evident they did not yet consider them to be *nos amis les ennemis,* as in 1814, but they had got so far as to look at them with relative calm and much inquisitiveness, and here and there two or three words were exchanged, with looks that were not unkind. The Germans generally were studiously civil, and even respectful; it was clear that stringent orders had been given them to put on their best behaviour. As one example of their conduct, I was told next day by a priest who lived in the Rue du Colysée—that is to say, within the occupied district—that nearly all the soldiers saluted him in the streets.

A Uhlan band was playing in the Place de la Concorde; the sun had set; evening was coming down; we were tired; so we went to dinner at the Hôtel, with the feeling that we had been through a memorable day.

Next morning, 2d March, several of us were out early, and wandered about for hours gazing at the sight of Paris "occupied." But though the spectacle was strange and (even to us foreigners) unpleasant, I cannot say that we perceived anything exciting. Furthermore, the novelty had worn off. The Germans had settled down, just as they had done in a hundred other towns throughout the war; they were in no way provoking in their atti- tude or conduct; and though the crowd of French onlookers was large in the morning and dense in the afternoon, no temper was exhibited (so far as I saw) on either side. The Parisian populace seemed to accept the situa- tion as a scarcely credible accident, disagree- able, though not, apparently, vividly afflictive.

The presence of the enemy was humiliating beyond doubt, but it offered a new sight to look at, and at all times the people of Paris like a sight, whatever be its nature. There was, of course, a strain in the air, a struggle between patriotism and curiosity, but it seemed to us Englishmen that curiosity had decidedly the best of it.

The day was fine; the Germans sat about in the streets, cleaning their arms, smoking, or staring at the mob. They did not look a bit like conquerors (as the world imagines a con-queror), and we all fancied that they were as astonished to see themselves there as the French were to behold them. At one moment we saw several couples of hussars waltzing gravely to their band on the central pavement of the Place de la Concorde (I must say the French did not like that at all—they had never done it them-selves); at another we watched artillery horses nibbling the bark off the trees at the Rond Point; then, again, we looked on at some open-air cooking by a Bavarian battalion in the Cours la Reine: but it was all quite peaceful, it did not seem like war, particularly in such sunlight. It was only at the limits of the occupied district, where German and French sentries faced each other, that there was anything acute to look at; to that sight we did not grow habituated, it was painful from first to last.

During the entire day we heard of only one dangerous incident. By the terms of the surrender the Germans had the right to enter the picture-galleries of the Louvre, and to cross the Tuileries Gardens for the purpose. But the French public was ignorant of the stipulation, and believed that the Place de la Concorde was the furthest limit allowed to the conquerors; so when it occurred to a certain number of Bavarians, who were inside the Louvre, to open the window of the Gallery of Apollo and to look out on to the Quai, the French who were passing there became naturally furious at what they supposed to be a scandalous abuse of force. A roar of rage went up from the crowd which gathered instantly below, to which the Bavarians replied by grinning and making faces. In five minutes a promising riot had worked itself up on the Quai, and stones began to be thrown at the window. Most luckily the headquarters of General Vinoy, who commanded the French garrison, were close by. He was told what was happening, despatched one officer to quiet down the mob, and another to General Kameke to beg him earnestly to withdraw all German soldiers from the Louvre and the Tuileries Gardens, declaring that the consequences might be disastrous if he did not. Most wisely— I think I may say most kindly—the German general gave way, and the German soldiers were ordered out. I saw nothing of all this, for at the time I was a mile off; but I heard about it an hour afterwards from a member of General Vinoy's staff, who declared that the German general had behaved very considerately, and had in all probability prevented an outbreak by abandoning his strict rights.

So the second day passed quite quietly.

In the evening I received the following note from a friend in the French Ministry for Foreign Affairs (I have preserved it as an historical document) :—

Les ratifications ont été échangées tantôt à Versailles. Les Prussiens évacuent Paris demain matin. Le Roi devait faire demain son entrée solennelle à Paris. Il a été désagréablement surpris de nous trouver en règle dès aujourd'hui.

This meant that, in consequence of the rapidity with which the assembly at Bordeaux had despatched their work of confirmation, the ratifications of the Treaty of Peace, which were not expected for some days—during which time the Germans were to remain in Paris—had reached Versailles that afternoon. The occupation had therefore to come to an end at once.

So, next morning, Oliphant and I started off once more to the Arch of Triumph; only, as the Champs Elysées were crammed with troops, we walked by the Boulevard Haussmann. On reaching the Faubourg St Honoré, at the bottom of the Avenue Friedland, we were stopped by the French cordon, and at the Rue de Tilsit were stopped again by the German pickets; but we had a pass for each, and got through. I believe I am correct in saying that we two were the sole spectators on the Place de l'Etoile, which was rigorously guarded on every side; at all events, we saw no one else, and most certainly we stood alone under the Arch.

The barricade had been demolished by the Germans, the trench had been filled up, the ground had been levelled, and the entire force strode through the great Arcade. If the march in was a failure, the march out was indeed a splendour.

As each regiment reached the circular enclosure, its colonel raised his sword and shouted the command to cheer, and then his men tore off their helmets, their busbies, or their czapkas, tossed them on their bayonets, their swords, or lances, and, heads flung back and eyes upturned in maddening excitement, and faces frantic with enthusiasm, they roared and yelled, and shrieked out hurrah! and gaped with wild laughter, as they marched on, at the names of the old defeats of Prussia chiselled on the stone above them—defeats which they were then effacing.

Some 40,000 of them poured beneath the Arch in utter intoxication of delight, exulting, triumphing. It was difficult to believe that the scene was real, so flaming was the paroxysm of rejoicing.

Oliphant and I grew hot as we gazed at that tremendous parade and hearkened to that prodigious pæan, and told each other, almost in a reverent whisper, that at last we knew what military glory meant. Never have I passed since in view of the Arch of Triumph without remembering vividly that soul-stirring spectacle.

When the last man was through and General Kameke's staff had closed the column, the dragoon sentries at the heads of the Avenues backed their horses in and formed a rear-guard, facing the howling mob which had followed the retiring army up the Champs Elysées. That mob pressed on, and whooped, and execrated, and defied. It was so easy to do all that at the tail of the occupation!

The German tread, the German march music, the German shouts, faded gradually out of hearing; there was a vast cloud of dust in the sunlight above the Neuilly road; and all was over.

Then came a cruel contrast. A picket of French soldiers, with lowered arms and faces full of shame, passed slowly through the crowd to reoccupy the Porte Maillot. The blouses remained masters of Paris, and, a fortnight later, made the Commune.

CHAPTER VII.

THE COMMUNE.

DURING the Commune of 1871 I was living
at what was then the top of the Boulevard
Malesherbes, exactly opposite the Park Monceau. The view from my fourth floor was
open and far-reaching — at that time it was
not masked by tall houses that have been
built since — it ranged from the hills of St
Germain on the right, past Mont Valérien,
round to the heights of Bellevue, Meudon, and
Sceaux, and to miles of the roofs of Paris away
to the left; in the middle, above the trees of
the park, the Arch of Triumph towered above
all. A better situation could scarcely have
been found for watching, safely and completely,
the various destructions that were going on.
And we had the view all to ourselves, for every
one who could run away had done so; people

who, from duty, had stopped in Paris for the first siege, went out of it for the second; the flat I lodged in was the only one inhabited throughout the Boulevard; the shutters of every other one were closed.

The bombardment from Mont Valérien and Montretout—which did far more harm than the innocent German fire had effected, smashed a quantity of houses in Auteuil, Passy, and the Porte Maillot district, knocked off nearly all the sculptures on the west side of the Arch of Triumph, and even sometimes damaged roofs and windows in the upper part of the Champs Elysées—did not reach into the Park Monceau. We were just out of range, and, after the first day or two, paid no more attention to the shells that went on bursting a few hundred yards in front of us than if they had been chestnuts cracking before a fire.

It was a dull and dirty time; but we were in satisfactory security. The Communards took money from the Bank of France and from such State institutions as had any, but there was scarcely any pillaging of houses. The Commune fought against the Government, but, with the exception of priests, who were objects of its special enmity, and of young men who refused to serve in its regiments, very few private individuals were molested.

Food of all sorts was abundant, for as Paris was besieged by the Versaillais on one - half only of its circumference, and as the outside of the other half was still held by the Germans, who had no motive for stopping the entry of provisions, supplies came in regularly through their lines.

The place was so safe that in my strolls about I was often accompanied by two little girls. I used to walk for mere exercise as a rule, for there was absolutely nothing of any interest to be seen in the part of Paris where I found myself. Indeed, during the entire duration of the Commune, I beheld, until the end came, but two remarkable sights.

One afternoon in the middle of May I was sitting reading, with the windows open. Suddenly the whole house shook violently, and a startling boom thundered through the air. I rushed out on to the balcony, and there, before me, clear-edged on the blue sky, stretched upwards from the house-tops a perpendicular cloud, hundreds of feet high, exactly the shape of a mighty balloon. From it broke out incessant fulminating reports, which sounded like the

crackling of musketry, but more deep-toned;
like the resonance of hammer-blows on iron,
but more rapid; like the roar of an express
train tearing through a station, but more lasting. And the sight was even grander than the
sound, for the cloud seemed made of countless
silvery ostrich feathers, rolling rapidly, con-
tinuously, almost regularly, round each other,
in and out, over and over, turning, twisting,
twining. The sun shone glowingly on the
whirling plumes; for a minute they revolved
in endless vortices, and then, softly, capriciously, began to change their hue; here they
whitened, there they blackened, elsewhere they
browned or yellowed; gradually they grew dim,
both in colour and in form; the convolutions
slackened; the clanging peal died down;
shapes dissolved; tints disappeared; movement stopped; sound ceased. The grand balloon lost life; it changed into almost ordinary
smoke, immense still, but inanimate; slowly its
edges melted, slowly rents appeared in it, slowly
patches drifted off from it. Another minute
and, excepting a few floating shreds, it had passed
away. It had, indeed, been a spectacle to see.

What was it? Of course it was an explosion
—but of what?

I ran down-stairs, found the *concierge* trembling, saw no one in the street, and started off towards the Seine, in the direction where the vanished cloud had stood. It was not till I reached the Pont de l'Alma that I learned the nature of the accident. The cartridge factory at Grenelle had blown up. The feathers were formed by millions of cartridges bursting in the air.

That was one of the two sights. The other was the pulling down of the Vendôme Column on 15th May.

I saw the Column fall from the same window near the bottom of the Rue de la Paix at which Laurence Oliphant had stood on 18th March (the day of the outbreak of the Commune), when a bullet coming through the glass, two inches from his head, brought him a message, as he told me an hour afterwards, that he was to leave Paris at once and go back to Mr Harris in America. The bullet was still in the wall.

At the foot of the Column the bronze sheathing had been partially stripped off, and the stone-work cut away to half its thickness, so as to facilitate breaking. Ropes had been laid on from the top to a windlass in the street. A long bed of fagots, twenty feet thick, had been prepared to receive the falling mass, and, in expectation of a great shock, every window in the neighbourhood had been pasted over with crossed slips of paper, so as to prevent fracture. The afternoon was fine; the crowd was great, though made up mainly of the small minority of the population which sympathised with the Commune: it filled every inch from the Rue de Rivoli to the Boulevard, excepting the Place Vendôme itself, which was reserved for the Communard authorities. A red flag had been fastened to the statue, and flew out in the breeze. About three o'clock the windlass was manned and the ropes hauled taut, and then began the effort to drag the column down; but, notwithstanding the chasm at its base, it held solidly, and would not move. Fiercely, but vainly, the strain at the bars went on. Suddenly, something smashed; the windlass flew back; half-a-dozen men were flung lumberingly into the air by the recoil; and the attempt in that shape had to be abandoned. After a delay of an hour, during which the stone was cut still further away, until the column at that point was pared down to about a quarter of its substance, longer ropes were procured, their ends were passed into the crowd, hundreds of eager hands laid hold of them, and once again the pull commenced, this time with direct traction.

I had got the statue into line with a chimney in the Rue Castiglione, so as to be able to detect the slightest oscillation; but there was none at all,—the column, all wounded as it was, stood immovable. Five minutes passed, five minutes of excited hope to me, for, from the braveness of the resistance, it almost seemed as if the destroying brutes would not be able to succeed. At last a shiver ran down my back; I had become conscious, after a particularly savage jerk on the ropes, that the line between the chimney and the statue was no longer exactly straight. Slowly— very slowly—the statue swerved past the chimney; slowly the great column bowed towards me —never did any one receive so superb a saluta- tion; slowly it descended, so slowly that it almost seemed to hesitate: in a great haze of spurting dust it fell. There was scarcely any noise, and no tremor of the air or ground; but the twenty feet of fagots were flattened down to nothing, and the dust rose thick like fog.

With a wild rush and frantic shouts, the people dashed past the sentries into the Place Vendôme, leaped upon the dislocated fragments, and howled coarse insults at them.

Mournfully I went away, murmuring to my-self, "Poor France!"

All the same, that, too, was a sight to see.

A few days afterwards, on Monday, 22d May, about seven in the morning, a servant rushed into my bedroom, and woke me with a shout of "Monsieur, Monsieur, the tricolour is on the Arch of Triumph!" I jumped to the window, and there it was. Its presence there, in the place of the red flag of the day before, could mean nothing else than that the Versailles troops had at last got inside Paris, and had advanced already as far as the Arch. In that case they might at any moment reach the Boulevard Males-herbes! That was indeed interesting.

I flung my clothes on and went on to the bal-cony. A dozen Communards in uniform were at that instant hurrying downwards past the house, looking nervously behind them as they went. I glanced all round, but nothing else was visible. It was not till several minutes had passed that I caught sight of something red moving between the shrubs of the Park Monceau. It was the trouser of a real French soldier: the troops were there. An officer, fol-lowed by a few men, came cautiously out from the trees, advanced to the entrance of the Park,

and looked down the Boulevard.   The instant
he was seen from below a dozen shots were fired
at him; the bullets whistled past us, high up.
I hastened down; but before I got to the door
three or four of the red trousers had run into
the roadway, had thrown themselves on their
faces, and had begun shooting down the hill in
answer to the Communards.   By this time firing
had become general throughout the neighbourhood; but its desultory weakness showed that
no serious resistance was being offered immediately round us.   By eight o'clock all the posts
of the Commune within a quarter of a mile of
us had been turned by other troops and evacu-
ated by their defenders, so that, excepting a
chance bullet travelling here or there over the
house-tops, we got out of immediate fire, and
were able to stand almost safely in the street.
As our house was the only one inhabited, the
wounded were brought in there, and an ambulance established in the courtyard, the men being
laid on carpets pulled off the staircase.   A surgeon
asked me to put up a Geneva flag at the door, to
make it known that doctoring was going on there;
so I ran up again and asked for something to
make a red cross.   The little girls tore up the
scarlet skirt of a big doll and pinned bands of

it on a napkin, which we nailed to a broom
handle. That flag hung out until, late in the
day, the ambulance was moved nearer the advanced posts.

In another hour the number of prisoners
massed on the pavement under guard had
grown so considerable that it became necessary to provide a temporary lock-up for them,
until cavalry arrived to supply an escort to
Versailles; the cellars of an unfinished house
close by were utilised for the purpose. I
spent the entire day in the courtyard of that
house, looking on at the coming in of the
constantly increasing crowd of prisoners — a
most curious and impressive exhibition, far
more interesting than the fighting. Some
cringed, some swaggered, some defied, some
cast themselves upon their knees and cried.
About one-tenth of them were women, who,
generally, were more violent than the men. A
few of them were wounded. On their arrival
in the courtyard their shirts were torn open
and their pockets turned out; the names they
chose to give were taken down (the list was
made so carelessly that future identification
was scarcely possible), and then, with much
brutality, they were thrust down into the

cellars. I remember many details, strange, sad, ridiculous, or odious, that would be worth telling; but I limit myself to a single case,— and I choose that one, not because it was more remarkable than a dozen others which came under my notice that day, but because I happened to be able to follow it out to what appeared to be its end, and can therefore narrate it completely.

About ten o'clock a young linesman staggered into the courtyard, bareheaded, ghastly pale, his tunic half stripped off. His neck was cut deeply open at the bottom of the right side for a length of nearly six inches, and the severed flesh hung down on to the shoulder in a thick scarlet fold; he dripped with blood, and, literally, spattered it about him as he reeled in. He still held his rifle with his left hand, and with the right he dragged after him a young woman with nothing on her but a torn chemise and uniform trousers (which indicated that she had been a *cantinière* of the Commune). With a last effort, the soldier flung the woman towards us, stammering out hoarsely, "She has killed my captain; she has killed two of my comrades; she has cut my throat; and yet I bring her to you alive!" And then the poor young fellow dropped heavily, his rifle ringing on the stones as it fell with him.

"Tie that woman's hands behind her," ordered the commanding officer, as the soldier was put upon a litter for conveyance to the ambulance. Silent and breathless stood the woman; she seemed to expect immediate death. Her shoulders, her tattered chemise, her arms and hands, were splashed everywhere with blood; the expression of her white face, with the hard glazed eyes, the clenched teeth, and the strained distortion of the corners of the mouth, was demoniacal. Straight she stood up before us, her head thrown back as if to dare the worst; she made no answer to the questions put to her. There was discussion amongst the officers as to whether it was not their duty to have her shot at once. But, though the case was clear, they shrank from commencing executions by a woman, and, after some hesitation, spared her, taking it for granted that, when tried, she would be condemned. Her arms bound back. she was sent into the cellar. She was, however, the only one let off; from that moment every prisoner, man or woman, brought in red-handed, was taken across to the Park and executed straight away.

At four in the afternoon the first column of prisoners was formed up outside to march down to Versailles. Under the pressure of many other violent sights, I had forgotten the murderess of the morning, and when, in the ascending stream of captives, she emerged from the dark staircase into the daylight, her appearance was so frightful that, for some seconds, I did not recognise her. She trickled with sweat, for the heat below had been terrific; the blood on her chemise and skin had dried into black cakes that stuck to her; her hair, dishevelled, hung in glued, glazed spikes, over her eyes; she had evidently been sobbing, and, as she could not move her hands, had been unable to wipe her face, which was scored with long dirty stripes formed by tears and perspiration, and looking like fresh scars of burns. We all stared at her with horror. "Wash down that woman," cried one of the officers. A stable-bucket full of water and a horse - sponge were brought, and a corporal sluiced her, with a bitter grin. She did not flinch one inch as the water was dashed in her face; exhausted as she must have been by fatigue, emotion, want of food, and the sickening atmosphere in which she had just passed six hours, she stood like a cliff: she shut her eyes and compressed her lips, that was all. Dripping, half-naked, horrible, she tottered out into the street and took her place in the column, to walk twelve miles. The cavalry escort formed up on the flanks. The colonel roared out to the prisoners: "Look here; if any one of you dares to attempt to leave the ranks he will instantly be shot down! Hats off. On to the ground your hats. Traitors like you march bareheaded. Hats on the ground, I tell you, or I'll fire into the heap of you!"

Five hundred hats and caps, of all sorts and shapes and colours, fell into the dust (to be picked up by the poor of the neighbourhood), and the wretched procession started.

Two months afterwards I was going through the prison of the women of the Commune at Versailles with General Appert, who then commanded there. In one of the long rooms thirty or forty women of all ages were sitting reading or working. At a table near a window was a young woman writing. She wore a neat brown dress, and had very bright well-dressed hair, and singularly delicate hands. A vague memory started in me. Surely I had met her somewhere. She was the murderess of 22d May! I had seen those white fingers of another colour; I had seen that hair less glossy and less combed. I stared at her for an instant, half-bewildered, half-horrified, and then asked General Appert to find out who she was. He called the matron and inquired. The answer came, "Oh, General, she is the best and quietest of them all, and really an educated person. The lady visitors are quite fond of her, she is so gentle and obedient. Of course there may have been some reason for sending her here; and, besides, it is suspicious that not a single friend has come to see her, and that we cannot find out who she is. But there is not the slightest evidence against her, nor even any imputation; so, as she is accused of nothing, she will, I expect, be set at liberty." As I listened, another voice came back to me. I heard a broken cry of "She has killed my captain; she has killed two of my comrades; she has cut my throat; and yet I bring her to you alive!" The poor boy who had stammered out those words was, in all probability, dead, and could bear no testimony. Ought I to interfere? I could only repeat what I had heard the soldier say, and that would have been no proof. The other witnesses of the scene were scattered, with their regiments, all over France. I held my tongue. The woman had perceived that she was noticed, and looked at me uneasily, with something of the fiendish expression I had seen in her face before. I heard no more of her, and have always supposed that she returned in peace to private life. Perhaps she married, had children, and loved them.

I may mention here that the majority of the prisoners were set free untried, from the same lack of evidence against them. Indeed, it could scarcely be otherwise, for it was impossible with such a mass of captives, collected under such conditions of disorder, and brought in so thickly, to write down in each case, with a view to future trial, the nature of the charge and the names of the witnesses. Futhermore, out of the 32,000 prisoners sent to Versailles a not inconsiderable proportion were innocent of all connection with the Commune, and were arrested by error or accident. I will give one example of the mistakes that happened.

In the next house to me an old coachman had been left, at the beginning of the first siege, to look after a horse. The horse had been seized by the authorities and eaten, so the man remained with nothing to do, waiting for the return of his master. I chatted with him sometimes, during the latter part of the Commune, as he stood smoking at the door, and a very decent old fellow he was. Well, one morning, during the fighting week, he was looking on at the formation, in the roadway, of a column of prisoners about to start, when he saw amongst them a groom, who was a friend of his. He stepped out to ask why he was there, and when, after speaking for a minute, he turned to come away, was thrust back into the column by the soldiers of the escort, who, seeing him amongst the prisoners, took him, not unnaturally perhaps, for one of them. He shouted in terror to the people on the pavement, many of whom knew him, and two or three of them rushed to the prison to look for me and to beg me to get the poor fellow released. It happened, however, that the officers on duty at that moment were strangers to me, and some minutes passed before I found any one to whom I could appeal. When at last a captain of infantry had consented to interfere, the column had started, and we had to run after it for some distance, and to parley with the commander of the rear-guard. Luckily he was good-natured: he listened to us pleasantly, believed my story, and had the man brought out and delivered up to me. But the shock had completely upset the poor old coachman; he could scarcely stand from emotion; he was got home and put to bed; after some days he became better, but remained really ill, his heart having become affected. He left Paris, without his wages, directly the trains began to run, and when last I heard of him, was dying in his native village.

Now I take up my story again on that Monday. The day passed amidst scenes of pain, absurdity, and ferocity; but there was intense interest in it all, it was human nature in a form which is not usually beheld, and I could not tear myself away. At last, however, the time for dinner came, and I went in to eat it. The little ones told me, with a mixture of awe and of the ignorant calm of children, that they had been watching the execution parties going across the road into the Park, and had listened to the reports of the rifles, especially to the *coup de grâce*, which seemed to have impressed them most. Happily, they had not seen the actual shooting, for it was hidden by the trees.

The next day, Tuesday, the same scenes continued.   Amongst the prisoners brought in during the morning was an Englishman, the charge against him being that he was wandering in the streets, and was unable to give an account of himself.   He could speak no French, so I was asked to question him.   He told me he was waiter in an eating-house for English grooms in the upper part of the Champs Elysées, and that the master (who had formerly been a trooper in the Life Guards) had stepped out of his door the afternoon before to look about him, in the belief that fighting round there was over, and had instantly been shot through the back by a sentry at the nearest street-corner.   The man had died in the night, and the widow had sent the waiter in the morning to the Batignolles, to take the news to a relation there.   There was a disregard of possibilities about this proceeding which indicated the state of mind of that widow.   I told the man that, according to the news we had, fighting was going on in every street of the Batignolles, that he might as well try to walk to the bottom of Vesuvius, and that he must go back. Thereon he asked me plaintively, " But, sir, can't I go to England at once?   I do so want to get out of this.   I am so frightened.   Is there a train?" I obtained for him a pass from the general of brigade, started him off again to the Champs Elysées, and hoped he got there.

That day the fighting seemed to thicken up again behind us: the Communards were defending themselves obstinately at a barricade in the Place Clichy, which was about 800 yards in our rear, and lost bullets began to come in at the back of our house. We stuffed the windows with mattresses, but the protection was incomplete. In the afternoon one of the little children was opening a glass door into the hall, when suddenly the pane above her smashed, and the splinters fell around her. Her first thought was that in some way she had broken it herself, and would be scolded; but it was seen at once that a plunging bullet had come through the top of the hall window above the mattress, had passed just over the child's head, had struck obliquely the glass panel of the opened door, and had cut itself in two on the sharp edge. The two halves of that bullet had fallen on the floor: the child picked them up and kept them. During the day forty-nine bullets got in at different windows of the house, but no one was touched. At night we had to lie down on the floor in the central corridor of the flat, so as to obtain protection from the walls.

But before we went to what we called our beds, the fires burst out.   At twelve o'clock we counted twenty-two distinct centres of conflagration in the vast area of roofs, though, of course, we could not tell exactly where they were.   The glare of the sky became so fierce that it seemed almost as if the atmosphere itself was burning. We gazed with consternation above us and below us at the universal furnace.   And the great rolling masses of reddened smoke increased the horror of the scene, for though they obscured somewhat the vividness of the flames and dimmed down their colours, they added a particular effect of lurid, lowering, looming awfulness, that could only be called hellish. And, as if all this were not enough, bullets went on crackling past us, and rang against the walls opposite, and clinked upon the housetops, and shells were bursting near, and broken glass and smashed stone and shivered slates were falling in the streets, and now and then a shriek of suffering arose.   It was not a night to be forgotten.

On the Wednesday morning a dense pall of smoke hung over Paris: the sun could not pierce it; the gloom was altogether special, unlike anything that fog produces, veiled, shaded, blurred, but not opaque, or even (properly) obscure. We saw the way about, but the way seemed unreal. And when, amidst that gloom, the news spread out that the Tuileries, the Hôtel de Ville, the Ministry of Finance, the Conseil d'Etat, and other buildings of all sorts, had been destroyed, there grew a rage amongst the peaceful portion of the population that made them scream for vengeance. They had been proud of their loved Paris, and much of their Paris was no more. They tried, in their fury, to lynch prisoners, and acts of cruelty were committed, under the impulse of wild rage, that are known only in times of civil war. I saw that morning five men led out for execution, their arms tied back; and, as they went, a crowd of women rushed at them, forced them on to their knees, struck them in the face, and spat at them. If the soldiers sent to shoot them had not rescued them, those women would have torn their hair off.

The close firing of the day and night before was over; the Communards had been driven back at every point. I heard that the Rue Royale was delivered, so, after breakfast, I went down to see. Notwithstanding the choking smoke, a considerable number of people had come out, and were staring, horror-struck, at the ruins. The killed on the Versailles side had been removed, but those of the Commune were still strewn about; and, here and there, a dead horse was being cut up into steaks by famished women, whose supplies of food had been stopped since the fighting began. The day passed in comparative quiet, for the nearest fighting was removed a mile from us.

In the evening I walked, with two officers off duty, along the Boulevard des Italiens. Of course there was no gas; the moon was hidden by the shroud of smoke; the shadows were so misty that they were scarcely recognisable, the lighted surfaces so dim that they brightened nothing. The ground was littered everywhere with smashed fragments from the houses, with broken glass, with leaves and branches shot off the trees, with paper torn from walls where the innumerable proclamations of the Commune had been posted up, with twisted bits of metal and sometimes abandoned arms. All this ruin crunched under our feet as we advanced along the centre of the roadway, in single file, five yards from each other, so as to offer smaller marks in the event of our being fired at. We got as far as the Rue Montmartre; but there we were stopped by officers, who told us it was impossible to go farther, because there was an untaken barricade in front. So back we came, utterly alone, staring round us at the murky sky, the dusky moon, the tattered trees, the shot-marked houses, and listening to the screeching of rifles, the grating jar of mitrailleuses, and the crackling of our own steps.

Could that be Paris? Were we, in reality, on the Boulevard des Italiens?

Several times the sentries at the street-corners called to me to join the *chaine* at the fires and help to pass the water-buckets (as was the usage then), but my companions answered for me and got me clear.

After this infernal scene the comparative stillness of the Boulevard Malesherbes was quite soothing. We walked slowly, talking of the day's work, and had got up nearly to my house, when one of the officers, gazing ahead, exclaimed, "Why, what's that? No, surely, it cannot be a cab!"

A cab in a street of Paris that night was about as probable as an ostrich on an iceberg; and yet a cab there really was, and at my door!

I stared at it in utter incomprehension. At that instant the *concierge* sauntered out, and I cried to him, "What is that cab doing here? Where on earth has it come from?"

"Gentleman just arrived for you, sir. He's gone up."

Never did I leap up-stairs so fast. My door was open: I rushed into the hall; and there, taking off an overcoat, was—Oliphant.

He had returned to England two days before from the United States, had stopped a few hours in London to arrange with the 'Times' to recommence his correspondence, and to get from the Foreign Office a despatch to carry to the Embassy as a sort of passport, and then he had come over with the intention of reaching Paris somehow. As the Gare du Nord was under fire that day, no train could enter, so he had been turned out at St Denis early in the afternoon. After some seeking he had discovered an adventurous cabman who, for money, was willing to run risks, had been driven, miles round, by Courbevoie, had managed to reach the Porte Maillot, had declared himself to the guard there as a special messenger to the British Embassy, and, at last, at ten o'clock, had reached the Arch of Triumph, to look down on Paris blazing. After filling his memory with that picture, he had turned to the left, and had come to me.

I told the cabman to find a stable somewhere, and then I gave Oliphant supper, which he needed badly, got a bed arranged for him, and talked to him till four.

Next morning I obtained a local pass from the general of division nearest us, and we two, after leaving the despatch at the Embassy, started off to try to reach the headquarters of General Vinoy, who commanded, under Marshal MacMahon, the army on the left bank of the Seine. Our object was to ask him, as old acquaintances, for two *permis de circulation* for all Paris, so as to be able to go anywhere, and escape the fire-*chaines*. We succeeded in our attempt, and we profited by the opportunity to see a good deal. One of the results was that we recognised very fully, from what we saw and heard, that if ever an army had sufficient reasons for relentless repression, it was on that occasion. It was said at the time, by outsiders, that it was monstrous to go on executing prisoners as was done that week. But, in all truth, the provocation was atrocious. Half the city was on fire, and the other half was more

or less destroyed; the fighting was furious; and
the shame of the whole proceeding was infinitely
augmented by its being performed under the
eyes of the German army, which rubbed its
hands with approval. Finally, and perhaps
more than all, the fierce blood of civil war
was up, and cruelties and vengeances were employed which, happily, are now unknown in
international war. Of the 14,000 Communards
killed that week, 8000 were executed; and at
the moment the softest-hearted of the spectators
declared it was not half enough.

On the Thursday evening the situation had
so far improved that a dozen Englishmen, who
had run over to see what was passing, managed
to get into the place. Some of them were
caught at once for the *chaines*, and were not
liberated until, drenched through, they had
passed buckets for some hours. Some went
about with us on the Friday. With one of
them (Mr Cartwright of Aynhoe) we had an
odd experience. We walked up the Rue Lafa-
yette until we got directly under the line of
bombardment from Montmartre, where Versailles batteries were established, to the Père
la Chaise, which was still held by the Communards. The shells flew over our heads some

hundred yards up, and we positively saw them pass! As their trajectory was high, and as we stood at the centre of the chord of the arc they described, our eyes had time to follow, and we perceived, at almost every shot, a black thread flash through the air.

On the Saturday morning Oliphant and I attempted a drive in the cab, and, showing our passes every five minutes, managed to make a real journey. We knew that the whole left bank of the Seine was cleared out, and we were assured (though incorrectly, as we found) that, on the right bank, fighting was continuing only in the quarters of Belleville and Père la Chaise. So we started down the Champs Elysées, past the Palais de l'Industrie, in the glass roof of which every pane seemed smashed, and made our first stoppage at the still burning Palace of the Legion of Honour, on the Quai d'Orsay, in order to peer into the cellars, where all the bedding from the Legion's schools at St Denis, Ecouen, and Les Loges had been piled up for safety before the siege. A thousand woollen mattresses, tightly stacked, had charred, in the absence of all draught, into a mass of silent, stagnant fire: it was strange that so vast and so intense a furnace (the heat of which was scarcely endurable, even at the distance where we stood) could be so still, so hushed, so peaceful: not a flicker could be seen, not a flutter could be heard; all was mute, motionless, white-hot smoulder.

Farther on, as we followed the quays, the signs of battle became more frequent, and again we got out of the cab to gaze about us. The bodies of several Communards had been thrown over the walls on to the river strand, to put them out of the way, and were lying there almost in the water. More dead horses were being cut up for food, and a horrible mess they made. People were out, but said they were afraid to leave their own immediate district.

At last we reached the Pont d'Austerlitz, crossed it, and became aware that we were nearing actual fighting. The shooting sounded closer, the dead were more numerous, and, from the fresh colour of the blood-pools round them, they seemed to have fallen recently. A sentry at the farther end of the bridge told us that the barricade there (round which we had diffi-culty in squeezing and lifting our cab) had only been carried that morning, and that at that moment the troops had not got beyond the Place de la Bastille, which was close by. As we emerged on to the Boulevard Contrescarpe, along the edge of the Canal, and caught sight of the spectacle it presented, Oliphant exclaimed, "A battle-field!" There must have been forty or fifty bodies there, lying, in some instances, so close together that our cab had to make zigzags to avoid driving over them. One man, on the pavement, had fallen on his hands and knees against a bench, and had stiffened in that position: his head hung down between his arms, and his long hair dangled on the ground. That sight upset our cabman; for a time he was unable to go on, and shut his eyes and trembled. "We shall have to put him inside, and do the driving ourselves," remarked Oliphant. But he got his nerves together, and managed to keep hold of the reins. As we neared the Place de la Bastille we saw, amidst thick smoke, half a battery of artillery, in position, firing down the Faubourg St Antoine, and an officer came running towards us, shouting furiously the order to stop. We showed our passes from General Vinoy, and asked to see the colonel in command, to whom we revealed our scheme of driving straight on and of returning westwards by the line of the inner Boulevards. He swore at us copiously, and told us, with exuberant exple-tives, that if we did not go back at once, he would send us, under arrest, to headquarters. We admitted afterwards that he had some justification for the view he took; but, at the moment, we were vexed, and thought him rude.

We had to return, humbly, by the way we had come; only when we reached the river we did not recross it, but remained on the north bank, turning to the right along the quays and into back streets, in nearly every one of which the paving-stones had been pulled up to form shelter-trenches or small barricades. The result was that the roadway was composed mainly of alternate wells and walls, into and over which we floundered, the cab bounding, tumbling, and straining tumultuously: why it did not smash up into molecules will remain for ever an unsolved mystery. At last we reached the burned Hôtel de Ville.

We stopped in the middle of the great Place, and stared. We were alone; not another soul was in sight. For the first few moments, in-stinctively, we drew somewhat away from each other, to avoid speaking in the presence of such lamentable ruin. We both felt that silence was the truest and most respectful sympathy we could offer. And when we did begin to talk, it was in a whisper. The destruction was terrific; but the desolation was more appalling than the destruction, and the solitude doubled the desolation. French hands had wrought that havoc, but there was not a Frenchman there to grieve. For some minutes we gazed sadly, and then the habit of action resumed its influence, and Oliphant, moving towards the gaping central gateway, said gently, "Let us go in."

Now, it might have been natural for firemen, in working uniform, to "go in" there; but it was absolutely unnatural that ordinary people with ordinary clothes should attempt to do so. The four outer walls, calcined, roofless, windowless, still served as an enclosure; but, so far as we could see, the entire interior had disappeared into confused heaps of broken, blackened, shapeless stones, charred timber, and bent iron. Such bits of inside walls as remained standing served merely as props for the piles of *débris* that leaned against them; half-melted gutterpipes, with long stalactites of lead that had chilled as it dropped, hung about like trellises; from every pore of the fuming wreck streamed up brown smoke; loosened fragments dropped and roused thick echoes,—that much we could perceive through the yawning openings: what more could we discover if we went in? But, all the same, we did go in.

As we emerged from under the scorched disjointed archway, a block of marble cornice fell, from somewhere, almost on to Oliphant. He jumped aside, exclaiming, "That was close!" We found our way barred at once, and in every direction, by steep tall slopes of riven pitchy stones; the smoke half stifled us; the heat was intense; our eyes were stung by the scorching dancing glimmer in the air. We looked about, apparently in vain, for a path to anywhere. At last Oliphant pointed to what looked like a cliff of coal, some twenty feet high, away in a shadow on our right, and said, "I think we could get up there." When we reached the foot of it, after scrambling over blocks, and bars, and chasms, we found that, like the rest, it was a nearly perpendicular declivity of cinders and smelted rubble, scorched, murky, burning hot, tottering, and slippery with greasy soot. It would have been awkward to get up, even if it had been clean; but with its covering of thick oily smut, it seemed almost unclimbable.

And yet we did climb up it. We burned our boots, we blacked our clothes, we bruised our knees, we chipped and broiled our hands; but we clambered to the summit of the incline, and, from the crest, looked down into what had been the famous inner court of the Hôtel de Ville, where had stood the *escalier d'honneur* and the glass cascade. It was a crater after an eruption, a vast fiercely ravined cavity of deadened fire. The smoke blew out of it in volcanic clouds, and inflamed our eyes and throats still more, and the stench sickened us. We were told afterwards that several Communards had got drunk in the cellars, had gone to sleep, and had been slowly grilled away amongst the embers. It was impossible to stop there—even Oliphant avowed that. We looked round intently, made a great effort to fix the scene upon our memories, and slid down, somehow, to the ground. We ran out into the open, took deep breaths of air, laughed at each other's grime, and drove straight home to clean ourselves.

Next day (Sunday, 28th May) the last defences of the Commune were stormed by the Versaillais, and the insurrection came to its end. That afternoon 6000 prisoners, in one column, guarded by several regiments of cavalry, were brought along the Boulevards on their way to Versailles. We stood, to see them pass, at the top of the Rue de la Paix, in an enormous crowd: all Paris had come out, exploding with satisfaction, to hoot the captives. I have looked on at many scenes of grievous misery and degradation, but never have I beheld any sight so strangely painful as that march past. The exceptional aspect of abasement of that mass of wretches arose from an altogether special cause. It was produced neither by the prostrate condition of many of the prisoners (several of whom could scarcely drag themselves along), nor by the hideous expression of most of their faces, nor by the merciless brutality with which they were treated by both the soldiers and the mob: it sprang from a totally different characteristic of the sight—a characteristic that nobody had ever beheld before, nor perhaps ever imagined. Almost every one of them had been forced to turn his coat inside out! It was the astonishing effect of that livery of shame, worn by such a mass of men at once, that rendered the scene so matchlessly abject: we two almost shivered as we stared at that spectacle of ignominy. We had not conceived it possible that vile dishonour could express itself so poignantly.

Even the grotesqueness of the parti-coloured sleeve-linings—many of the pairs being of different stuffs and colours, and nearly all of them in rags—was lamentable, not laughable. And yet, after all, notwithstanding the extraordinarily repulsive features of that piebald procession, it cannot be denied that it was a fitting and illustrative ending to the odious and imbecile Commune.

On the Monday morning I walked with Mr Cartwright along the line of the fortifications from the Porte Maillot to the Point du Jour, at the end of Auteuil, in order to see the damage done by the bombardment. The smashing had occurred capriciously: some houses had almost escaped; others were carried away down to the very ground; others again had fronts or sides shot off, but were otherwise little injured. In two cases, where the *façades* alone had disappeared, the furniture of four floors was still standing almost undisturbed in the opened rooms as in a doll's house. But the general total of destruction, considerable and widespread as it was, seemed relatively small when we considered that it was the result of several weeks of continuous shelling. The fortifications themselves were not much knocked about, though, in places, the ground behind them was ploughed deeply.

The cleaning up of Paris, which commenced on the Sunday, directly after the passage of the prisoners, was pretty well completed by the Monday night. The rapidity with which it was performed astonished everybody: it was only achieved because everybody helped. Of course certain signs of fighting remained visible; but the barricades, the holes, the fallen trees, the dirt, vanished in twenty-four hours. The dead were carted off; the paving-stones were laid back roughly in their places; the rubbish was swept into heaps. The sensation of delivery was so keen amongst the population that they almost rejoiced.

I terminate these recollections by quoting a curious definition of the Commune, given to me by a man whose name is known in England, but whose words have been heard by few Englishmen.

About the middle of June, Oliphant's mother and Mr Harris arrived together in Paris from America. Mr Harris remained there for three months, during which period he conveyed to me, with the assumption of inspiration which was proper to him, a certain number of remarkably expressed opinions. One of them described the Commune as "a yell from the lower man; an up-seething from the turbid sources; a snatch at the impossible and the undefined; a failure where success would have meant a nation's shame."

CHAPTER VIII.

MR WORTH.

TOWARDS the end of August 1871, I listened one night to a conversation between particularly competent persons about the probable effects of the war on the trade and prosperity of France. Most of the talkers were convinced that, just as, by an unvarying natural law, the number of births increases always, in every land, after a sudden reduction of population by disease or battle, so would the general commerce of France enter rapidly into a period of remarkable activity, to make up for the year just lost. As concerned Paris in particular there was, however, less hopefulness: it was argued that the trades of Paris were, in the main, of an altogether special nature; that they ministered almost entirely to artificial needs; that their marked characteristic was to supply the unnecessary and even the frivolous; that ornaments, artificial flowers, the varied details of clothing, furniture, what the Germans call "gallantry wares," and *articles de Paris*, interesting as they were as local products, scarcely counted amongst the real elements of the national dealings of France; and that, in consequence, there was no sufficient reason for anticipating that Paris would share proportionately in the prompt revival of ordinary business which was predicted confidently for the rest of the country.[1]

As I walked home I thought over all this, and the more I thought the more the subject stretched. All sorts of additional ideas started up; my fancies grew wider and clearer; after branching in several directions they assumed suddenly a specific shape. I asked myself what had been the effect of the war on the most conspicuous, the most widely ramified, the most labour-employing of all the unnecessary industries of Paris—on dressmaking?

The answer came almost at the same instant as the question. A scheme evolved itself in my head. I would get up the subject, and would write an article for 'Blackwood' on "The

---

[1] This gloomy expectation was not realised; the trade of Paris recovered as quickly as that of the nation at large.

Influence of the Siege of Paris on the Art and Trade of Dressmaking"! I would inaugurate the study of the psychology of women's gowns in their relation to both international and civil war! What an utterly new idea!

That was the result to be attained. The means I devised for achieving it were fully worthy of so grand an end. I would go next day to Mr Worth himself for the requisite information!

The fact that I was a total stranger to Mr Worth did not seem to me a difficulty : I felt scarcely any hesitation at the idea of thrusting myself upon him. I had been told, it is true, that he was as busy as a Cabinet Minister; that it was more difficult to obtain an audience from him than from a reigning sovereign ; that he was a loftier personage, by far, than any living poet. But there were considerations of another nature which encouraged me to hope that I should vanquish all these obstacles, that I should succeed, in spite of them, in obtaining admission to his presence, and that, once there, he would condescend to answer my audacious questions.

Those considerations were that if ever there was a real public man, a veritable figurehead of his day, a man who, all by himself, represented a great contemporaneous fact, it was precisely Mr Worth. In his sole person he was the complete realisation, not only of the artistic theory and the commercial practice of women's dress, but also (I supposed at least) of its abstract essence and hidden meanings; he incarnated the matter, the morality, and the philosophy of the problem. He was all this so completely that the perfection of his success had enabled him to win the infinitely rare distinction of bestowing his name on his period: just as history talks of "the age of Pericles," of "the Augustan era," of "the times of the Medici," and of "le siècle de Louis Quatorze," so also had I often heard the Second Empire described as "l'époque de Worth." In such a position he surely owed himself to the world, especially to humble inquirers like myself who sought simply to sit at his feet and listen to his words of wisdom. The more I reflected on these elements of the situation, the more did I incline to the impression that, indiscreet as I might be in troubling him, he would scarcely say no, and that he would not shield himself remorselessly behind what was then called in the French Chamber "the wall of private life." His personality was too great, too dominating, too full of public responsibilities, to permit him to refuse to enlighten his generation on such a virgin question as the connection between frocks and battles.

To inspire myself with still more courage, I quoted aloud the words of the Persian poem, "The moon looks on many night-flowers; but the night-flowers see only one moon." Mr Worth was the moon; I was one of the night-flowers; surely the moon would not decline to shine on me if I appealed to it for a ray.

In the morning I prepared a list of interrogatories. At five o'clock I walked into the first floor of No. 5 Rue de la Paix.

Mr Worth was in. I sent my card to him. Within five minutes he was standing before me!

I said to him, "Forgive me for disturbing you. I know how occupied you are, and yet I have come to ask for an hour of your time. I want to write an article on the influence of the war on the dressmaking trade of Paris. Such an article would, I am sure, be read with interest, in the present condition of public feeling. You typify, for everybody, the entire idea of Paris dressmaking. I want to ask you questions. Will you kindly listen to them? Will you, still more kindly, answer them?"

He stared curiously (perhaps rather suspiciously) at me, hesitated for a few seconds, and then said rapidly—

"Yes. I shall be very pleased to have a chat with you, and to tell you what I can. I never was asked about such things as that. But we can't talk here. At this instant seventeen persons are waiting for me in nine rooms. Come to dine with me to-morrow at my country house. Take the 6.30 train from St Lazare to Suresnes. My son will meet you at the station and will show you the way. *A demain.* Glad to make your acquaintance. Of course you won't dress."

I went away delighted. The great man had not repelled my venturesome demand; on the contrary he had admitted it, not only benignantly, but with a cordiality which filled me with hopes.

Next day, at seven, I got out of the train at Suresnes. On the platform I found waiting for me a very good-looking, charmingly-mannered young man, who introduced himself as Mr Worth *fils* (he is now the head of the firm, I believe), and in his agreeable company I walked to the great red brick château. He told me that his father had not arrived from Paris, but that he would be down directly. This was so true that, before I had passed a minute on the terrace gazing at the view over the Bois towards Paris, I heard the gallop of a horse tearing up the hill, and Mr Worth, spattered with mud and foam, rode in at the gate. He had come down, he said, in a quarter of an hour.

We stood chatting for a couple of minutes, and then he turned to the house to change his clothes.

At the same instant I saw appear on the verandah a lady in white. Her elegance, her grace, her winningness were such that I stood still in admiration.

"My wife," observed Mr Worth. "Let me introduce you to her."

Now, I had heard from public rumour that Mr Worth, when he was cutter at Gagelin's shop in the Rue de Richelieu, had married one of the young persons employed there. I had heard additionally, from the same source of information, that Madame Worth, with the adaptability of many of her race, had fitted herself admirably to her new situation, and had become in everything a lady. But, though I had seen many transformations of that nature, no previous experience had prepared me for what I beheld at that moment. With the ease of an accomplished woman of the world, with combined dignity and simplicity, with infinite gentleness of movement, she made two steps towards me, smiling graciously, bowing slightly, welcome on her face. She wore a high but short-sleeved white satin dress, striped with bands of black velvet; a profusion of lace hung over her; long Suède gloves reached almost to her shoulders; two or three bracelets were on her arms; a diamond was half hidden here and there in the lace. Never did white satin appear to me to be so completely absorbed into the person of its wearer; she and her gown were so absolutely one that, for months afterwards, Madame Worth and white satin presented themselves to my thoughts as synonymous, simultaneous, identical, unseverable. I could neither disjoin them, nor conceive one without the other. All other women in white satin appeared to me impostors. It never occurred to me, as I looked at her, that such a gown was at all out of place, where no one else was dressed. She was Madame Worth: her name purported dress; who on earth should wear white satin, even at six o'clock in the morning, if she did not? Her right to the extremest elegancies of raiment, to the most excessive daintinesses of finish, was more complete than that of any other woman whatever. Besides, she was so sympathetically attractive and had so grand an air that the dress was, after all, merely one of the details of her presence. With all this I noticed instantly that she, a Frenchwoman, had a charm that was distinctly Spanish, far more Spanish than Slav (the only two purely national types of charm) ; so Spanish, indeed, was it—of the fair variety—that if I had seen her in the drawing-room of a great house, and had been told she was the Marquesa de la Vega de Granada, daughter of the Conde Duque de Valladolid y de Burgos, I should have thought the statement perfectly natural.

As her husband went into the house, she turned to stroll with me on the terrace, saying, in a soft voice, " I hear you want Mr Worth to give you information about the effect of the siege upon our business. He will be very pleased to do so, and I hope you will let me read what you write about it."

I triumphed! I was making the acquaintance of this most delightful woman; I was acquiring a totally new perception of the possibilities and the meanings of white satin; and I was about to be instructed, by the greatest master in the world, in the mysteries of the psychological relationship between gowns and politics, fashions and sieges, women's vanities and wars! What a success my projected article would have! Who ever had such good fortune!

The conversation, however, was not active. The delightful woman was a little silent: I perceived, during the evening, that it seemed to be her practice to leave talking to her husband. But what a delicate picture of a delicate woman! I remembered Napoleon's exclamation, "Nothing on earth is so pretty as a woman in white in a garden!" I agreed entirely with Napoleon.

Presently Mr Worth came out again, in a rusty brown jacket and a battered straw hat without a crown; whereon it occurred to me that Madame Worth was dressed for both of them (and, indeed, for all of us), which still further explained the white satin.

We dined (Mr Worth keeping on the crownless straw hat at table) in a vast greenhouse which seemed to cover an acre of surface, amidst a forest of palm-leaves, tree-ferns, variegated verdures, and fantastic flowers. Some quiet persons, who did not speak, and who, I gathered, were relations from the country, joined us at dinner. There was a perplexing mixture of patriarchal simplicity and of the assertiveness of modern money, of thoroughly natural unaffectedness and of showy surroundings, of total carelessness in some things and of infinite white satin in others, which was so new to me that, at first, I felt a little bewildered, and wondered whether I was dining with Haroun al Raschid in one of the disguises he so often wore.

After the soup, Mr Worth began, " Now put your queries.   I am ready."

I commenced my speech. I explained that my original object had been to obtain materials for an article for " Maga " on the effects produced by the war on Paris dressmaking; but that he and his wife had received me with such kindness that I felt emboldened to extend my questions, and that, with his permission, I would ask also for information on the metaphysical aspects of dressmaking; on the influence of dress on the formation of women's character; on its share in constituting their natures in different lands; on the motives, impulses, temptations provoked by it; on the moral effects of dress; concerning which most interesting elements of the subject, he, of all men, was most capable to instruct me.

"Hum," said Mr Worth, when I had finished. "I don't quite follow you in all that. I never thought of it in that way. The war has done me harm, of course, as it has done harm to everybody. I have lost a year by it; but I daresay I shall pick up again, for orders are coming in very fast. But as to all those other things you mention, I shall have to think a bit. Influence of dress on women's character? Why what, exactly, do you mean?"

"To put the matter, to begin with, in a narrower form, With what object do women dress?"

"What a question!" laughed Mr Worth. "Do you mean to say you don't know? Why, women dress, of course, for two reasons: for the pleasure of making themselves smart, and for the still greater joy of snuffing out the others."

"And never for their own persons only? Never to frame in and set up their individuality by clothing it in what befits it best? Never to harmonise their essence with their substance, their self with their surroundings?"

"I must say again that I don't quite follow you. If you mean whether they dress to suit their bodies, according to their own ideas of suitability, I should say no at once; because, you see, the women who come to me want to ask for my ideas, not to follow out their own. They deliver themselves to me in confidence, and I decide for them; that makes them happy. If I tell them they are suited, they need no further evidence. My signature to their gown suffices!"

"Do you never find a rebel amongst them? Does no one ever claim the right of personal invention and choice?"

"Choice? Yes, certainly; but only between my various suggestions. And very few do even that; most of them leave it all to me. But as for invention, no. My business is not only to execute but especially to invent. My invention is the secret of my success. I don't want people to invent for themselves; if they did, I should lose half my trade."

Madame Worth looked affectionately at her husband (they seemed to be a most attached couple); then turned to me, raised her finger to her forehead, and said, "It is here, you know; here lies the secret of his success!"

I went on all the same, "What a pity it is you will not enlighten me as to the influence of dress on character!"

"I tell you I don't see it," answered Mr Worth. "Perhaps I'm too busy to have time to make observations of that sort. I've a deal to do, you know: I've twelve hundred people in my employment, who need some looking after; and I can't stop on the roadside to pick flowers. I thought it was about the war that you wanted to know?"

"So I do. But the truth is, the subject grows upon me. As I talk to you, I see more and more in it. If I were not afraid of being indiscreet, I should put a hundred questions to you about its endless developments. The whole thing grows bigger to me as I sit opposite you and imagine all that you must know about it."

"Oh, of course, I do know a good deal, but it's all personal. There's the subject of payments, for instance,—a very big subject indeed, from my point of view. Then there are the jealousies, and the envies, and the hatings, and the love-makings. Oh, I know a quantity about all that. Is that what you mean?"

"No, no; not that at all. That is, as you say, personal. That would not interest English readers. What I am looking for is general: I want to discover what are the great principles which govern the action of dress in the constitution of feminine temperaments and the guidance of feminine conduct."

"I suspect I know more about all that than my husband does," put in Madame Worth, laughing.

"Ah, but it is I, not you, who am being examined," retorted Mr Worth, laughing still more; "and I mean to keep the answering to myself." Then turning to me, he went on. "Now, suppose I tell it all to you in a personal form, then you could stitch it together in a general form, and so make a gown of it your-self—I mean an article."

"Really, I'm afraid I couldn't manage that," was my reply. "I shouldn't feel justified in building arguments on individual facts, each one of which might be exceptional. If I am to set forth the effects of this war on one of the most important branches of the trade of Paris, and, more particularly, if I am to try to analyse the interaction of dress and character in women, I must have your direct pilot-age on every point and your authority to quote your opinion. My own fancies would be ab-solutely valueless without your aid; at the best they would be nothing more than the pins with which you fasten stuffs together."

"But I'm ready to tell you everything—that I know. Only I suspect I don't knów. Those 'developments' you alluded to just now are rather outside my day's work. And yet I should really like to tell you if I could. Let me try what some of my stories will do for you. When you have heard them you can decide whether they are of any use."

Whereon for half an hour he narrated tales which, assuredly, were excessively amusing, but were of no sort of use for the purposes I had in view.

At last I ventured to put in an interruption and to ask, "Now, out of all that, what is your impression (to take one single point) as to the average amount which women spend on dress?"

"There is no average at all. How could there be? In every case the expenditure is individual, and is governed by circumstances. There are quantities of very respectable women in Paris who don't spend more than £60 a-year on their toilet, and who, for that sort of type, really don't look bad. But you mean, of course, the women who come to me, who are of a different class. Well, they get through anything you like, from a minimum of £400 to a maximum of £4000. I know several women who reach somewhere about £4000; not every year the same sum—sometimes more, sometimes less. Why, some of them—especially Russians—need £150 a-year for shoes alone, without counting boots."

"Are the Russians more extravagant, then, than all the others?"

"It doesn't run in nations, exactly. Often it's a Russian, as I say, or it's an American. Sometimes it's a Peruvian or a Chilian; sometimes, even, it's a Frenchwoman, though the French are usually rather careful; economy is in the blood, you know. Here and there a Spaniard or a Southern Italian may turn prodigal, or people of some of the outlying races. But rarely does an Englishwoman get really wasteful, and I have not known a single case of a German reaching any such amount as I am talking of. Some of the Americans are great spenders; all of them (all of them that I see, I mean) love dress, even if they are not extravagant over it. And I like to dress them, for, as I say occasionally, 'they have faith, figures, and francs,'—faith to believe in me, figures that I can put into shape, francs to pay my bills. Yes, I like to dress Americans."

I was beginning to despair somewhat, but I

went on, persistingly, "You said just now that orders are coming in very fast. Am I to infer that, according to your present impression, your branch of the commerce of Paris will rally rapidly from the blow the war gave it?"

"Oh, certainly. I haven't a doubt about it. Women can't do without new clothes: they may deprive themselves of all sorts of other things, but they won't shut off that one. They can't. I'm quite sure that, by the end of the year, we shall be going on as if nothing had happened. Payments will be, for a time, more difficult to get in—French payments, I mean; foreign payments are not affected by the war— but trade itself will become as active as ever."

"Two nights ago I heard the contrary opinion expressed. It was argued that, as the main object of the work of Paris is to supply the unnecessary and the frivolous, that work will not be resumed rapidly."

"Who were the silly people that said that? Why, it is precisely the unnecessary and the frivolous that everybody comes to buy in Paris. People don't travel from everywhere to the Boulevards in order to lay in stocks of timber, or raw sugar, or ships' ballast."

"Ah, my dear Mr Worth," I exclaimed, with delight, "now you're coming to the philosophy of the thing. That is just one of the points I want you to comment upon. Go on; pray go on."

"Philosophy? it's self-evident reality. There's no philosophy in it—not a bit. Do you ever hear of a woman—or a man, either—who did come here for anything but the unnecessary?"

"Perhaps not. But, you see, that is exactly what I should like you to show me in its detailed application to dressmaking."

"I will. Here are some of my experiences in proof of it."

And he went on for another half-hour pouring out a second series of diverting stories, all bearing, certainly, on the energetic pursuit of the unnecessary by clients of his, but with not one word in them that I could utilise.

The cruel impression grew in me that my proposed article would never be written, from the unexpected impossibility of obtaining the necessary information. Yet I struggled on, and asked again—

"But, once more, about the effects of the war? Do I gather quite correctly that, in your opinion, it will not exercise any durably injurious effect on the dressmaking trade?"

"That is my opinion, certainly. I have already said so. We have lost a year, and that can never be recovered. But, from the nature of things, the war will bring about no permanent change in women's wants. The future will be like the past, excepting, of course, that (unless there is a Restoration of some sort) there will be, from the disappearance of a Court, less brilliancy in Paris itself, and less demand here for extreme elegance. So far as I am concerned, however, I expect that foreign orders will make up for what I may lose here. That's all."

I echoed mournfully, "That's all! Then if we can't get any further in that direction, let me look again, if you will permit me, at the metaphysical aspects of the subject. When women order dresses, are they enthusiastic or indifferent? Does the process fill them with emotion, as if it were a highly exciting ceremony; or do they perform it as if they didn't care?"

"That depends. Beginners are almost always stirred up. Clients who come to me for the first time show generally very perceptible flutter. But habit quiets that; after a time they cease to be fussy, and take things quietly. Your question means, I suppose—judging from what you have said about the moral effects of dress on women—whether the ordering of new gowns is a cause of deep palpitation to them. I answer that by saying that they pass through two stages: at first, as a rule, according to my experience, they are distinctly agitated; afterwards they become calm. But always, no matter at what age, the discussion of the composition of a new dress fills every one of them with joy. I will give you some examples."

Then he began a third series of gossipy tales, which lasted for another half-hour (he certainly had a great liking for personal stories, and a great stock of them, and he told them vividly). But, as before, there was nothing in them that could be made instructive.

It became evident to me that I had failed. My expectations were not—and were not destined to be—realised. I had met most pleasant persons; I had listened to many diverting experiences of a strange sort; I had had a glimpse into the inside of a life that was new to me; but I had obtained nothing of what I came to seek. I was very disappointed. I had been treated, however, with such kindness, that I felt it would be ungrateful to allow my disappointment to show itself. So I chatted on as if I were delighted.

"What a charming house this is, and what a collection of beautiful things you have in it!" I exclaimed, trying a new direction of thought.

"I'm glad you like it," answered Mr Worth. "The ladies who come down here to tea—clients, you know—are all good enough to say it pleases them. By the way, would you like to hear some stories of my tea-parties?"

"Thanks very much," I replied; "I am afraid they would scarcely fit in with what I want to do. Besides, the hours have passed so quickly that we have almost reached the moment when I must go to catch my train. I thank you very warmly for your charming hospitality, and for all that you have told me, though I fear that I shall scarcely be able to build much on it."

"Well, if you do write anything, you will let me see it. Of course you will not repeat any of the anecdotes I have told you; they are confidential, you know."

I took leave of them all with renewed thanks, with the sentiment that I had made acquaintance with excellent people and that I had passed a very interesting evening, and with a strong addition to my many previous reasons for knowing that the best-planned and best-intentioned efforts often fail.

I thought a good deal about it all in the train; I thought a good deal more during the days that followed; but I did not attempt to write the article, for I had nothing to put into it.

Shortly afterwards I went away for some months. I never met any of the Worths again. But I have always remembered them, and I remember them still, with hearty sympathy and with sincere gratitude for their most kind reception of me.

CHAPTER IX.

GENERAL BOULANGER.

NOTORIETY needs usually time to grow; it is
only in rare cases that it sprouts abruptly.
Even General Boulanger, who acquired a prodigious quantity of it, did not rush upon the
world between night and morning. It is true
that, when his moment came, he burst out
eruptively, but he had to pass previously
through a period of preparation: several
months elapsed, after he was first heard of
in Paris, before he became a personage. In
1885 the papers began to mention an unknown general called Boulanger, who held a
command at Tunis, and who had made himself conspicuous there by a noisy quarrel with
somebody. No notice was taken, however,
of the name, until it was announced, additionally, that this same general had so ingratiated

himself with the Radical party that he was certain to be taken up and pushed on by them. Even then most people continued to be unaware of his existence. But it ceased to be possible to go on ignoring it, for he was thrust forward so determinedly by the Left—who at that time imagined they had found in him a man after their own heart—that, at the beginning of 1886, M. de Freycinet, chief of the Cabinet of the day, was forced to appoint him Minister of War.

A "legend" began instantly to form; rumours, assertions, fables filled the air with strange rapidity; within a week of the nomination everybody professed to know everything about the new - comer; every mouth was crammed with news; the town buzzed and blazed with fantastic details. Notoriety detonated at last with a deafening roar: its fuse had been burning slowly up for months, but when the explosion came it was tremendous. People stopped each other in the street to add something wonderful to the heap of wild tidings. To quiet French natures (of which there are a good many) the situation became a sudden nuisance; to the foreign looker-on it brought out, vividly and amusingly, the *gobe - mouche* tendencies of the large minority. This acquaintance whispered to you, with profound conviction, "We have got a man at last." That one murmured, with still deeper earnestness, "I tell you—I know it for a fact, though I cannot mention my authority — that he is capable of everything, will do everything, and will succeed in everything." A third, with mystery, intensity, and awfulness, pointed to the sky and muttered, "The day is coming! Revenge and victory!" Others, again, a good many others — but they were all, of course, Conservatives — declared that this untried general was simply an additional danger; that he was choked with ambition, vanity, and presumption; and that he would lead his country to destruction. So, on one side, it was asserted that a saviour had arisen for France (I wonder if I could count up the various "saviours" I have heard of there); and, on the other, it was alleged, with equal infallibility, that a fresh and vast peril was looming in the sky. And these two absolutely opposite affirmations were expressed about the same man by a quantity of people, not one of whom knew anything whatever about him, excepting what they read in the papers or heard from each other, and not one of whom had ever seen him.

The question of getting a sight of him, of perceiving him in his real person, and otherwise than by his photograph (which was in every shop-window), was discussed widely, but uselessly. Everybody, in each of the two camps, was excitedly curious to behold him; but the curiosity remained unsatisfied, for the general hid himself behind the walls of his Ministry. Excepting at the Chamber, where, occasionally, he made red-hot Republican speeches which were cheered delightedly by the Left, he was not to be discovered. He was said to be working so overwhelmingly at the entire reorganisation of the army and the War Office, and at gigantic projects for re-constituting France and Europe, that he had neither time nor patience for mere worldly gatherings. Even in the Bois in the morning he was not amongst the riders.

Naturally, this invisibility stimulated still further the gaping eagerness of the public, and if it was adopted for the purpose (as very probably it was) it succeeded admirably. The "legend" that had leaped up round the name of Boulanger was swollen daily by reports (usually in the minutest detail) of what the unperceivable general was doing, of the universal changes he was effecting, and by vague but prodigious hopes aroused by the action that was attributed to him. A French army at Berlin, the Koenigsplatz column of victory transported to Paris and set up as a trophy in front of the Madeleine, were talked of by the most enthusiastic as possibilities of an early future. Imagination rioted. The supposed artificer of all these dreams was sought everywhere and found nowhere; but the crowd grew more and more convinced that he was nurturing astonishments and hatching history in his laborious seclusion. If, by accident or obligation, he did go anywhere, it was solely to official houses; for, in consequence of the rupture between society and the Republic, functionaries are rarely seen in private drawing - rooms. Now, as official houses mean only those of French Ministers and of foreign diplomatists, it was in the latter alone that people of society (who never set their feet in the former) could hope to satisfy their inquisitiveness about the new man. It was amusing to hear them put earnest questions about the chance of meeting him at this embassy or that legation, and to observe what a gathering there was at any place where it was imagined he might appear. This excitement contributed most fertilisingly to the growth of the earlier constituents of his ephemeral reputation.

Like the people round me, I became curious too. It was indeed scarcely possible to remain indifferent on a question which, in some shape or degree, was agitating everybody. But though I went about expressly to look for the new general, I never happened to encounter him indoors until he had been for more than three months in office. I had, it is true, perceived him in the Chamber, and had heard him speak there; but that view of him was of no use, for as French Ministers, when sitting in their places in Parliament, turn their backs to the public, and as, when in the Tribune, they are acting a special part, I could not base any opinion on such insufficient evidence.

At last I received an invitation to meet him at dinner, and commenced on that occasion the slight and superficial personal acquaintance I had with him. When he was announced, a quiet man came in at the door, with eyes that, at a distance, looked mild, without a symptom of either the vaunting arrogance which I had heard imputed to him by his enemies, or of the commanding superiority which was attributed to him by his friends. He showed no vulgarity and no forwardness, no energy and no signs of character. His manner, watched from five yards off, seemed gentle and unpretending. He looked so thoroughly nobody that, if I had not known who he was, I should have turned my eyes away from him with indifference. My first impression, at a distance, was that there was absolutely nothing in him.

Oddly enough, I chanced at table to sit next to a lady who belonged to a family of soldiers, who was thoroughly acquainted with the history of General Boulanger, and who told me more intimate details about him than I had heard before. After describing to me many circumstances of his career and conduct, she went on to say that he was known in the army as a *metteur en scène;* that he could do nothing simply; that he had always an extraordinary faculty of getting himself remarked and of compelling notice; that he succeeded in giving an appearance of studied effect to his most insignificant proceedings, so much so that it was said of him by his comrades, "Oh, that fellow! he has a way of his own for doing everything: even if he gets wounded in action, he manages it so as to attract attention." This description was not only much more analytical and psychological than anything I had heard before, but it seemed also far more likely to be exactly true.

In the evening I was introduced to the General, had some talk with him, and examined him attentively, with the result that I had to alter my first impression about him. The mouth, which in vainglorious faces is the most tell-tale feature, was concealed by the moustache and beard; but its divulging action was performed for it by a peculiar and singularly self-conscious movement of the muscles of the upper part of the cheeks, which corresponded, necessarily, to analogous workings of the invisible lips. The eyes, which had seemed to me so placid—almost dreamy, indeed—at a distant view, were filled to overflowing, when seen close, with a contented but transcendent conceit, which at moments became positively glaring. He was evidently not at his ease; the shield of indifference behind which he tried to shelter himself concealed nothing; the need of self-assertion pushed it aside continually, and the real man stood visible.

The physiognomy, the ways, the movements, fitted thoroughly to the bad side of his reputation, and I had to recognise that I had judged him too advantageously on his arrival. Seen from far, and seen from near, there were two different persons in him. The eyes, above all, at that moment of his career when, around him, all was clamorous popularity, and when, before him, all was hope, were astonishingly suggestive of aggressive vanity; and yet, notwithstanding this, the expression, on the whole, was weak—indeed its feebleness was as clearly indicated as its conceit. It is true that the two usually go together.

Still, though I regarded him after dinner far less favourably than before, I could not help making excuses for him. He had jumped with violent abruptness, unprepared by character or by previous contact with the political or social world, to the highest position open to a French soldier; he had become master of the army, and a figure before Europe; his situation and his reputed power as a statesman were boiling higher every day; the destinies of his country were supposed to lie in his hands, and a portion of the nation was looking up to him as a heaven-sent leader to the glorious unknown.

In all this there was enough, and a good deal more than enough, to spur on a vain nature, and to turn a feeble head. He had been taken up as a tool by others, and had committed the not unnatural mistake of imagining that he was capable of working for his own hand. He had extenuating circumstances in his favour, supplied by the folly of many of his own countrymen, whose adulation he was impotent to resist. The mixture in his face of shallowness and self-sufficiency explained the man. From that first meeting with him I had a strong suspicion that his ambition, whatever might be its extent, would be neutralised by the indecision of his character.

After that dinner I met him from time to time, and had occasional short talks with him. He touched on many subjects, but he did not seem solidly acquainted with any of them, and had no brilliancy of conversation. He inspired me, more and more, with the conviction that his dominating need was to show off, without any accompanying consciousness that he would be found out if he went beyond his depth. I watched him with amusement, but with little real interest, and saw, in almost each of his words and acts, unceasing preoccupation about the effect he was producing. He was almost always surrounded, at the evening gatherings where I met him, by a circle of flatterers and starers. He had ample opportunities for satisfying his longing to be remarked; and I used to wonder what there could be in him to explain his success. The more he struggled to conceal his vanity and to appear indifferent, the more did he show his innate self-assertion; at least, that was the impression which grew stronger in me each time I saw him. He was irritable, too, and especially could not support the semblance of a contradiction: he was convinced, apparently, that it was everybody's duty to agree humbly with so great a personage as he had become. He did try, I think, to behave with a certain *bonhomie*, but it was not natural. It seemed that a voice was always coming out of him, proclaiming, "I am the future!" And yet, with all this, he was at moments almost sympathetic: he did not possess charm, but he could be what the French call *câlin*, and when occasionally he took the trouble to be so, he became agreeable.

He was not liked by women, many of whom professed to be afraid of him and avoided him; indeed, at that period of his career, I rarely saw him talk to women,—it was only later that a few of them began to offer him attentions. His main object then appeared to be to influence men, and, on the whole, he succeeded amazingly in doing so.

One night at the Elysée (where, at the open receptions, almost anybody with a tail-coat could go in), the General was, as usual, in the middle of a gazing group. Suddenly he grew tired of being stared at and commentated, turned sharp round, and walked rapidly into another room. I happened to come up just at the moment, and found myself for an instant next to a middle-aged man, who, from his appearance, was probably a small provincial functionary or trader, brought there by the deputy of his arrondissement to see the show. The man followed Boulanger with his eyes, as he vanished in the crowd, and said aloud, just as I passed by, with the aggrieved air of a sight-seer robbed of his spectacle, "Well, a fellow who runs away like that won't lead others when the time comes." Those words came back to me afterwards when the General had not only failed to lead others, but had run away again himself.

On another occasion, elsewhere, a friend to whom I was talking said to me, as we looked across the room at Boulanger, "We modern French have become a nation of idolaters. It is absurd to go on calling us Christians. We are always eager to worship a new god, provided he shines, and only so long as he shines. When he grows dim we smash him." At that instant some one at my side said "Bon soir" to me. I turned and saw M. de Lesseps. For him, too, I had sad reason to remember, later on, the words, "When our god grows dim we smash him." It was a strange coincidence that he should have appeared that night just as they were spoken.

So things marched on until the 14th July, the great day of Boulanger's life, so far as popular admiration and exterior manifestations were concerned. It was the date of the review of the army of Paris, held every year by the Minister of War of the moment, on the race-course in the Bois de Boulogne. And it was also the date of the appearance of Boulanger's black horse—the horse that became, for the time, a party symbol, a political finger-post, a feature in the history of France. He was a prodigiously showy horse, as gorgeous as he was famous; he was composed principally of a brandishing tail, a new-moon neck, a looking-glass skin, and the action of Demosthenes. He seemed to possess two paces only, a fretting walk and a windmill canter. He was a thorough specimen of what the Spaniards call "an arrogant horse": he was gaudy, yet solemn; strutting, yet stately; flaunting, yet majestic; magniloquent, yet eloquent. He was drilled with the most admirable skill; his manners were so superlative that, with all his firework display, he could not have been either difficult to handle or tiring to sit. Never was a horse so emphatically suited to his rider: the two were identical in their ways; each was as gilded as the other. As the horse bounded along before the troops, the General (who had a weak grip) rocked on him; at every stride he swung harmoniously in the saddle, and bent right and left alternately, like a stage sovereign bowing to his assembled people. The entire pageant was wonderfully got up .for its purpose, with the rarest perfection of both preparation and execution. The man, the horse, the ribbons and stars, the white feathers, the plunging and the swinging, were all exactly what they ought to have been to delight and fascinate the mob. The means were so triumphantly appropriated to the end, that two hundred thousand spectators screamed themselves sore with rabid enthusiasm. They flamed with frantic raving. That soldier and that horse incarnated so livingly the popular idea of glory, that every soul in the long lines of crowd grew utterly demented. The yelling became, from minute to minute, more and more furiously mad. And the General, feeling that his work was good, rocked, swung, and smiled, then smiled, swung, and rocked, and took his place for the march past.

Around me, in the tribune where I sat, the feeling was of another nature. I was in a group of widely experienced people, who were all particularly competent to form and express opinions about conduct, to judge of the fitness of means, and to appreciate the value of results; and their impressions were, almost unanimously, strongly hostile to the performance we were beholding. Two or three of us argued against the others, that we had before us a pretender, who was appearing for the first time in official splendour before the population he desired to subjugate; that, knowing unmistakably how to strike the imagination of that population, he adopted processes consummately adapted to that purpose; that being intimately aware of the peculiar appetites of the fish he wanted to catch, he threw to it the very fly it longed to swallow; and that, in consequence of all this, his flashy meretricious acting, though in the most deplorable taste in the eyes of men and women of the world, was entirely in situation towards the mass. We urged that we were looking at a play, which must be measured as a play, and that we were outside real life, the rules of which had no application to the extravaganza represented before us. The exhibition in itself was of course mere vulgar ostentation, like a Court procession in the theatre of a fair; but the political effect which was manifestly produced by it seemed to us to constitute, under the special circumstances of the case, some excuse for the tawdry details of the display. The majority, however, would not listen to us; the mummery was too offensive to them,—they could see in it nothing but its bedizened swagger.

When the last regiment had gone by, another act of the piece commenced. The General turned his horse round, and, alone, came plunging and rocking across the few hundred yards of turf which stretched between him and the tribunes. He increased his speed as he got near, dashed through the opening in the rails, and pulled up sharp, all foam and feathers, in front of M. Grévy, saluting as he halted.

This beat the crowd, and broke them; it was more than they could stand. Wildly they rushed in from everywhere, disregarding sentries and policemen, and came tearing towards us, waving hats and handkerchiefs, cheering, shrieking, roaring, as if Boulanger were the one joy of their lives. Howling thousands filled, in half a minute, the whole space in front of the Presidential tribune; in the midst of them the General rocked softly, and did his best (though very unsuccessfully) to look indifferent. As I was in the next tribune, and watched him with a glass, I was able to follow all the movements of his expression: he tried to hide his delight, but it was too much for him, and became distinctly visible. He really might be pardoned for being unable to conceal it, for the moment was full of throbbing triumph for him. People round me called him hard names — "buffoon," "circus - rider," "charlatan," "impostor" — but, though the epithets were justified superficially, the personal side of all this swaggering almost disappeared for me, as I have already said, behind the wonderful management of its public effects.   It was impossible not to blame the man; it was equally impossible, according to my view, not to recognise that the pretender was doing well.

The scene lasted for five minutes, and then the President of the Republic—who was utterly obliterated, and looked intensely sulky—took his place gloomily in his carriage.   The General put the black horse at its side, and, under pretext of respectfully escorting M. Grévy, supplied the people with an opportunity of yelling, "Vive Boulanger; c'est Boulanger qu'il nous faut!" from Longchamp to the Elysée.   Such frenzied bravos, such outcries of enthusiasm, had not been heard in Paris since the army came back from Italy in 1859.

As the procession started, some one near me exclaimed bitterly, "And that man is to be the master of France!"

About the origin of the black horse I was told five different stories—all, I presume, equally false, but of each of which I was assured by the teller that it alone was true.   The first was that he was bought out of a circus in Roumania; the second, that a Paris dealer discovered him at a sale in Yorkshire; the third, that he was the charger of a very big lieutenant of cuirassiers, and was not up to the weight; the fourth, that he was a cast-off from a racing stable; the fifth, that he was the pick of the riding-master's horses in the cavalry school at Saumur. In each case it was added that he had been brought to Paris three months before, had been ridden regularly with troops, and had had his paces finished in one of the regimental *manéges* in Paris, where Boulanger had mounted him daily for the preceding fortnight, to get accustomed to him. I repeat these tales to show the curiosity that was felt about the horse: he was regarded for a time as a national institution, and a portion of the community felt proud of him.

A few days after the review I quitted Paris, and did not see the General again until the winter, when I met him at the German Embassy. I thought him changed. He seemed grave; responsibility and struggle had begun to mark him. But, all the same, the double look of weakness and conceit was in his eyes, as evident as before. When I caught sight of him he was leaning against the piano, Count Münster towering over him as they chatted together; a thick ring of gazers was around them.

The General put on, as usual, unconsciousness under the staring; but it was evident that he felt it, probably because, on that occasion, the starers were of a class to which he was not quite accustomed: many of them were, of course, of other nationalities. The curiosity about him had become almost more ardent than at first, in consequence of the still growing belief that he had a destiny before him; but amongst those whose business it was to watch him and to form a reasoned judgment on him, an increasing minority was convinced that he was a bag of wind.

Of the political motives and processes of General Boulanger I say nothing. The gossip of Paris was full of them, and, like others, I heard a good deal—true or false—about them; but they, like the circumstances of his private life, lie outside the present subject. At the time it was, of course, impossible to separate the man from his political intentions and acts, for the good reason that he became what he was precisely because of the intentions and acts attributed to him. They enabled him to place himself obtrusively in front of every one else in France, and yet nobody could explain why he got there, otherwise than because he thrust himself forward, and because, for the moment, nobody pulled him back. Never did self-assertion produce more abundant or more immediate effects. Each time I looked at him, during that winter, there came into my head the two famous lines in the ' Biglow Papers ':—

" I do believe in humbug general-ly,
    Because I find it is a thing that has a solid vally."

In his case humbug had indeed a "solid vally." Humbug lifted him so near to personal power, that if he had had the pluck to snatch at it when it seemed ripe to his hand, he would, in all probability, have seized it. Whether he would have held it is a different matter.

But his humbug, enormous as it was, appeared to me to be unconscious: it guided him, I fancy, in everything; yet, according to my impression of him, he was unaware of it. Here is an example to explain my meaning. Talking one night of Napoleon, he said: "A great mind, yes; a great man, no. A soldier, a lawgiver, an administrator, in the very highest meanings of the terms; but nullified by impetuosity and vanity. No man can be truly great unless he knows when to stop." Thereon he glanced round, as if he expected one of the listeners to answer, "As you would, General." It happened, however, that everybody remained silent. So he went on: "Alexander the Great stopped at the Hyphasis, and turned his back on India. It was for that act of prodigious self-control that posterity confirmed his epithet of Great, which it has not accorded to Napoleon. I tell you, gentlemen, real greatness consists in self-restraint." And he looked round again.

If he, of all men, could express such opinions, it was, I fully believe, because he honestly thought that they applied truthfully to himself. I never suspected him of being a wilful dissembler, for I never saw in him a sign of intentional deception. He was too blindly vain to be able to imagine that he needed to employ artifice. He was intensely content to be what he was; was convinced that he was great; and did not conceive that he had to prove it. That is what I want to convey in saying that his humbug was unconscious. Others may have judged him otherwise,—I am only saying what I thought myself.

In the spring of 1887 I met him, for the last time, at a gathering at the Spanish Embassy; and there three or four French ladies grouped themselves round him, sat with him, and talked to him intimately. The rest kept off and disapproved; but it was a commencement, and the General was palpably pleased by the feminine attentions of which he was beginning to be the object. Flattery in a social form was supposed to be new to him, and to have, for that reason, all the more attraction for him. If only he had lasted long enough, a little Court would, I doubt not, have formed itself around him, in hopes of what he might some day become.

But neither the flatterers nor the flattered were destined to continue their respective parts, for, in May, the Cabinet was upset, and the General, after sixteen months of office, had to give up the Ministry of War. From that moment his official position in Paris was at an end, he ceased to be invited anywhere, and I had no more opportunities of meeting him, or even of looking at him, excepting at the Chamber and in the street.

In July 1887 he was appointed to the command of the 13th Corps, at Clermont. The scene at the Gare de Lyon, on the night of his departure for his post (when, very possibly, he might, if he had dared, have made himself master of France); his indiscipline and disobedience; his condemnation to thirty days' arrest in his quarters; his deprivation of his command in 1888; his career as a Deputy; the fierce opposition commenced against him; his flight; his exile; and his miserable death,—all lie beyond my bounds. I limit myself to the little I personally saw of him. The rest is public history.

I add only a story from the 'Figaro,' about the arrest, as an example of the manner in which everything serves to make a *mot* in France. The railway trains stop at Clermont for five minutes, and passengers are informed of the halt by the usual cry of "Clermont, Clermont; cinq minutes d'arrêt!" The 'Figaro' pretended, while the General was in confinement, that the guards and porters were so affected by his misfortune that, in their emotion, they shouted instinctively and unconsciously, "Clermont, Clermont; trente jours d'arrêts!"

General Boulanger began explosively, and finished shatteredly: it may indeed be said of him that he was "hoist with his own petard." He knew how to dazzle a mob, but not how to win power. As my neighbour at the dinner when I first met him told me, he was essentially a *metteur en scène*, but when he had produced the *scène* his faculties were exhausted. He was aspiring and personally brave; but, as developments of his vanity, he was nervous, bad-tempered, mutinous, seditious, infirm of purpose, and without moral daring. He commenced so brilliantly and ended so deplorably that, out of pity for his fall, much may be forgiven him. I have the liveliest recollection of his faults (especially of those which I saw him commit); but I cannot help regretting his fate.

CHAPTER X.

THE OPERA.

THERE are subjects which seem, by their inherent nature, to be necessarily full of incidents; from which everybody, as a matter of course, expects impressions; but which are so fundamentally deceptive that, when they are looked at closely, scarcely anything can be discovered in them. It would be going too far to pretend that their water turns into sand and their flowers into ashes, but it is certainly true of them that they promise in theory enormously more than they fulfil in practice, and that they dazzle on their surface and deceive in their substance. The Opera is — according to my experience at least — one of the most delusive of this class of subjects: it holds out all sorts of tempting expectations, and realises scarcely any of them. Though my recollections of the Paris Opera extend over nearly half a century, they form, in the main, only a confused heap, with splashes of colour here and there, but without much outline; it is with difficulty that I can detect amongst them an occasional clearly marked picture. Until I began to look into them with the purpose of describing them, I always took it for granted that they contained a quantity of strange details and amusing memories, and yet, on careful examination, I find them comparatively empty of any well-defined sensations. Such few details in them as may be worth narrating are all small. The retrospect disappoints me. The reason is, evidently, that, like others, I have gone habitually to the Opera as a mere social act, just as I should go into a drawing-room, and have sought for my diversion there in the boxes rather than in the performance. To the people who constitute society (or who think they do) the Opera has always meant, and still means, the house rather than the stage. To see and to discuss acquaintances, and to be seen and discussed by them, and (for men) to go gossiping from box to box, are everywhere the main objects with which "the world" goes to the

Opera. In southern Europe, indeed, it may be said that they are the sole objects. There are, of course, a quantity of people, less regular in their attendance, whose purpose is simply to hear the music; but they are not "the world." They do not talk, as others do. In Paris, especially, it is an accepted principle that society *n'écoute que le ballet*. It is only when the curtain rises on the short skirts that tongues grow still and that eyes turn unanimously to the stage. There are, naturally, singers to whom everybody listens, and songs (even if heard for the hundredth time) for which all conversations are interrupted; but the general rule remains, that relative silence and attention are reserved, in Paris, for the dancing. Of a spectacle so constituted there is much of personal tittle-tattle to narrate, but there is very little of general interest; and that is, I apprehend, the reason why people who have frequented the Opera during nearly all their lives find, as I have just said, so little to tell about it.

This condition of the question is reflected in the copious literature which exists about the Paris Opera, for it does not give a quarter of its pages to the music, and concerns itself principally with the ballet. There are quantities of volumes, dating from various years of the century, filled largely with biographies and adventures of *danseuses*,—their variegated loves, their vanities, and their bitter jealousies of each other are described minutely; but there are scarcely any ordinary books (I exclude, of course, the special and technical ones) which treat mainly of the music performed, and not one, so far as I know, which describes the public and its ways.

And yet the chronicles of the boxes are precisely what society cares most about, because they mean the history of a not inconsiderable portion of the brighter social life of Paris. As those chronicles, if they existed, would of course be purely local, foreign readers would not care for them; but to Paris itself they would signify "the Opera," almost to the exclusion of all else. When it is remembered that there are three subscribers' nights each week; that very few of the *abonnés* possess a box for more than one of the three nights (sometimes, even, for only one night in a fortnight); that there are in the present house about eighty boxes open to subscription, on the ground tier, grand tier, and second tier (the side-boxes on the second tier are left for the miscellaneous public, who also have all the boxes at their disposal on the off-nights), it will be perceived that the number of different subscribers is considerable, and that the intimate history of each box is very varied and altogether special to itself. The controllers on the staircase must need some training before they get to know the face of every one, as undoubtedly they do. No subscriber's box is ever let; it is lent to friends when not used by its owner: in the event of mourning or long absence it may be leased away for an entire year; but it would be against the usages of Paris to retail it for money for a single night. The difficulty of obtaining an *abonnement* is very great, for a box once got is held solidly in a family. When the old Marquis de Casa Riera, who had for many years the great Entre Colonnes box on the right side (for which he paid, if I remember rightly, £1200 a-year, and which, though he was blind, he filled every night with pretty women), died some fifteen years ago, there was a hot flutter of excitement in the Paris of the Opera as to what would become of the succession to the box. After a palpitating struggle of influences, efforts, and diplomacy, equal in emotion to the contest between Ulysses and the Telamonian Ajax for the armour of

Achilles, the nephew and heir of the old Marquis managed to keep the box for ône night a-week (he could not obtain more), and it was won for each of the other nights by persons of the highest place, who had been longing for it impatiently for years. An ordinary box for one night a - week costs from £240 to £320 a-year, according to its size and situation. The combat for boxes is unceasing: it is one of the features of the rich life of Paris, and, to those who know the people and the circumstances, the combat is diverting to watch. Nothing, however, need be told about it here. I presume that it has gone on from the beginning, in every one of the thirteen houses in which the Paris Opera has successively been lodged; but it is naturally more acute at present than it ever was before, for the two reasons that more and more people are able to pay for a box, and that the present theatre is so superb that it acts temptingly and stimulatingly on the ambitious. Amongst its other glories it is by very far the biggest that exists; for instance, it is about three times the size (in surface and in cube) of the Operas of Munich and St Petersburg, and about ten times greater than that at Berlin.

The influence of the Paris Opera on the

history and development of operatic representations has been considerable; no other city has
contributed in the same degree to the founda-
tion and the progress of both opera and ballet.
In Opéra Comique particularly, as distinguished
from the Italian Opera Buffa, the French have
taken the lead from the commencement; it is
to them, almost alone, that we owe the growth
of this branch of composition, the representation
of which, however, has been transferred from
the Grand Opera to smaller houses. Of course
the first operas were, as the name shows, Italian,
and the earliest of them are said to belong to the
end of the fifteenth century. But the establishment of what is now understood by a national
Opera was a purely French act, and dates from
1671, when "Pomone," a "*Comédie française en
musique*," was performed, under the management
of the Abbé Perrier, in a house built for the
purpose, in what is now the Rue Mazarine.
In 1672 Lulli was appointed by Louis XIV.,
through the protection of Madame de Monte-
span, Director of the Opera, and the title of
"Académie royale de Musique" was bestowed
on the undertaking. From that time to this
there has been a French Opera in Paris.

But though the French Opera has always been a national institution, and though all its productions have been in the French language (excepting when, once or twice, an Italian troupe has given momentary representations), its destinies have been largely shaped by foreigners. From Lulli to Gluck and Piccini, and from them again to Rossini and Meyerbeer, foreign composers have contributed as much as Frenchmen to its success. Futhermore, it must be remarked, as a characteristic of its history, that almost every one of the early pieces, whether by French or foreign composers, contained a ballet; indeed, on looking over the long list of *Tragédies lyriques* and *Pastorales* represented during the first hundred years, scarcely any example can be found of song without dance. And the dancing was an important portion of the whole show, not a mere *divertissement* as in our day. This feature was as clearly marked from the origin as was the cosmopolitan composition of the music. In the first letters-patent which Louis XIV. addressed to the management of the Opera, he used words which painted clearly the state of the opinion which then existed as to the importance of dancing.

He said :—

Bien que l'art de la danse ait toujours été reconnu l'un des plus honnêtes et des plus nécessaires à former le corps, néanmoins il s'est, pendant les désordres et la confusion des dernières guerres, introduit dans le dit art, comme en tous autres, un grand nombre d'abus capables de les porter à leur ruine irréparable. . . . Beaucoup d'ignorants ont tâché de le défigurer et de le corrompre en la personne de la plus grande partie des gens de qualité. . . . Ce qui fait que nous en voyons peu, dans notre cour et suite, capables et en état d'entrer dans nos ballets, quelque dessein que nous eussions de les y appeler. A quoi étant nécessaire de pourvoir, et désirant rétablir le dit art dans sa perfection et l'augmenter autant que faire se pourra, nous avons jugé à propos d'établir dans notre bonne ville de Paris une Académie royale de danse, composée de treize des plus expérimentés du dit art.

So that the Opera dancing-school was regarded in the royal mind as an aid for the development of Court dancing. And yet, notwithstanding this enthusiasm for "*le dit art,*" it was not until 1681, after the princesses and ladies of the Court had set at St Germain the example of dancing and declaiming before the King in the ballet "Le Triomphe de l'Amour," that women dancers ventured to show themselves on the public stage. Until then the female parts in the ballets had been performed by men. Emboldened, and indeed authorised, by the initiative from above, Mademoiselle La Fontaine had the courage to appear as a *danseuse* at the Opera; she was the first woman-dancer, the originator and creator of the profession; and as she had the good fortune to commence her career just at the right moment, she had immense success and made her name immortal. Whereon, it may be observed that immortality amongst mortals is obtainable sometimes from curious sources.

At that time dancing was regarded as such a noble act that not only did the bearers of the royal and historic names of France perform before the sovereign, and not only did the King himself take part sometimes in person, but, additionally, a young Prince Dietrichstein, the eldest son of the then Grand Master of the Imperial Court at Vienna, positively danced a *pas seul* in public on the stage of the Paris Opera on 19th June 1682, in the lyric tragedy of " Persée." The ' Mercure Galant ' (the famous monthly journal of the time) described the scene in detail, saying, amongst other things, "Ce jeune seigneur, qui n'a pris leçon que depuis un an, dansa cette entrée d'une manière si juste qu'il fut admiré de tout le monde." Yet, notwithstanding the success of the attempt, a hundred and fifty years passed before persons of society appeared again as dancers on the Opera stage. In 1833, when Auber's opera of "Gustave III." was produced, the ball scene, with its splendours and its mad galop, produced such an effect on the audience that, as a contemporary writer puts it—

Il y eut entre la scène et la salle un fluide de communication et d'attraction tellement impérieux que la scène se peupla au préjudice de la salle. Des dames —de grandes dames—affublées de dominos épais, le visage couvert d'un masque impénétrable, vinrent galoper au milieu des danseuses et des figurantes du corps de ballet. Les hommes suivirent l'example des femmes; ils passèrent sur le théâtre; et, un certain jour du carnaval, les lions des avant-scènes et de l'orchestre, déguisés en ours blancs et noirs, conduisirent le galop à la grande joie d'une salle comble.

To give another example, of a different sort, of the importance acquired formerly by the ballet, I mention the fact that when the first Vestris, founder of the dynasty and father of "*le Dieu de la danse*," declared, with profound conviction, "there are only three great men in the world, myself, Voltaire, and the King

of Prussia," nobody seems to have felt surprise
or to have offered contradiction.

The portraits of twenty of the most famous
danseuses are to be seen in the *foyer de la danse*
of the present Opera House, where, from Mademoiselle La Fontaine down to Madame Rosati,
including Sallé, Camargo, Guimard, Noblet,
Taglioni, Duvernay, Elssler, Carlotta Grisi,
and Cerrito, a fairly complete gallery of faces
and costumes, reproduced from old pictures,
is on the walls. It is a curious collection
of the types and fashions of the two last
centuries.

The *foyer de la danse* was in other days a very
famous gathering-place. Regular subscribers
and distinguished personages alone had the
right to enter it, and for a long while the right
was regarded as a privilege. But since the
new house has been opened the privilege has
lost much of its ancient value. The *foyer* of
the former building in the Rue Le Pelletier was
old-fashioned, badly lighted, with faded velvet
benches, and with damaged frames to the mirrors; its sole ornament was a marble bust of
Guimard. And yet all Paris and all Europe (I
need scarcely explain that I am speaking of men
only) flocked to it as a place of delight. It was

full of traditions and associations; the history of recent dance was represented in it; every *danseuse* of name since 1821 (when the house was built, after the murder of the Duc de Berri in the preceding establishment in the Place Louvois) had received in it the homage of her admirers; with all its shabbiness it shone, with all its dinginess it glittered; it offered to its *habitués* what they considered to be a delightful pastime, and constituted a drawing-room of an intensely specialised sort.   The *foyer* of the new house is a vast gorgeous hall, all marble columns, brilliant lustres, endless looking-glasses, pictures, and bright ornaments: it is as magnificent as the old one was squalid; and yet it lacks the meaning and the attraction of the other, and is comparatively abandoned. The fashion has changed; foreign princes have ceased to think that their first visit to Paris has been incomplete if they have not seen it, and have not listened to the oracles of the priestesses of the shrine.   There is still a crowd in it (as thick, perhaps, as ever) during the *entr'actes* of the ballet; but the composition of the assem-blage is altered: it is no longer made up prin-cipally of ambassadors, ministers, and bearers of great names; journalists and Bourse speculators are abundant in it now. The young ladies, who have acquired from long practice the faculty of standing about unconcernedly and imperviously in draughts, with bare legs, arms, and shoulders, and with "des robes qui ne commencent qu'à peine et finissent tout de suite" (another definition is, "des robes excessivement hautes par le bas et excessivement basses par le haut"), do not charm the gentlemen of to-day as they fascinated their fathers. The *foyer* lives upon its ancient fame, and is still curious to look at; but it has fallen from the high place which once belonged to it in the life of Paris. When I first saw it, the gathering was in its full glory. Almost miserable as was the room, with its dirty sloping floor (corresponding with the incline of the stage), its low ceiling, and its air of general discomfort, the scenes that went on in it, the words that were spoken in it, and the people that frequented it, were absolutely apart; nothing like them was to be found elsewhere. The mixture of brilliancy, of elegance, of dance, of sparkling talk (on the side of the men), of love-making and of laughter, was prodigious. Neither natural nor experimental chemistry has ever produced a more intimate compound of fantastic elements: it was social and moral synthesis in its intensest form.   At that time the *habitués* of the *foyer* were convinced that they could not live without it; it had become necessary to their lives.   The present generation manages to subsist away from it.

Scarcely any of the stories told of *danseuses* are amusing; few of the heroines have left behind them any reputation of *esprit*.   The best known of the legends is that Mademoiselle Guimard determined, when she was young, that she would postpone growing old; so she had her portrait taken at the age of twenty, placed the picture on her dressing‑table by the side of her glass, and painted herself up to it every morning until she was fifty.   By that means she remained twenty during thirty years.   It was she too, who, at sixty, consented to give a final representation for her friends, on condition that the curtain should be kept down to the level of her waist, and that the spectators should see nothing of her but her legs, which, although her body was so thin that she was called "the skeleton of grace," had retained in age the beauty of their youthful form.

Of all the others there is not a story to be told, not one at least that is worth telling; the quartz contains no gold.   But yet there is something to be said of one of them. There was a dancer of whom it is impossible not to speak, not indeed to tell stories of her, for I know none, but to give her the first place which belongs to her in dance history—Taglioni! Nature did not, most certainly, intend that she should dance (although she belonged to a family of dancers), for, as a child, she was a most wretched object, pale, crooked, wasted; but will and work made of her a wonder. Her *début* was at Vienna; her success, however, was won in Paris, and Paris claims her as its own. She appeared there in 1827, but it was not till 1830 that, in "Le Dieu et la Bayadère," she took her real place. In 1832 came "La Sylphide," a still greater triumph, in which even the physical defects of Taglioni, especially her phenomenal thinness, seemed almost to add to the effect she produced:—

Elle devenait une ombre; elle se condensait en vapeur; elle flottait sur le lac bleuâtre et sous l'écume de la cascade, comme un flocon de brume soulevé par le vent! Une couronne de volubilis idéal s'enroulait dans ses cheveux, et derrière ses épaules frêles palpitaient deux petites ailes de plumes de paon. Sa robe semblait taillée dans le crêpe des libellules, et son soulier dans le corolle d'un lis. Elle apparaissait et s'évanouissait comme une vision impalpable.

She made diaphanousness the fashion; "toutes les femmes essayèrent *de se vaporiser*, à l'aide de jupes de tulle, de mousseline, et de tarlatane; le blanc fut presque la seule couleur adoptée." The dance of Taglioni was a revelation of new possibilities: it did not look human; she floated; when she soared into the air there seemed to be no reason why she should come down again; her bounds were the flights of a bird. She has had no successor; stage-dancing has become acrobatic; it is no longer the dream of grace which she had made of it. As she ceased in 1837 to dance in Paris (in consequence, I think, of some dispute with the management), it was in London that I saw her. She was not only extraordinary, but incredible; there was no believing that such aerial movements could be performed by a woman.

I leave the ballet where I found it, in the *foyer de la danse*, its now half-abandoned home. My object in referring once more to that *foyer* is to observe that, while everybody went to it, nobody but musicians ever looked, or do look, into the *foyer du chant*. Singers, unlike dancers, fear cold air, and stay in their dressing-rooms until the last moment; if they appear at all in their *foyer*, they are so wrapped up that they are in no way smart.

I have but two or three disjointed details to tell of them, for the stories about singers are even rarer than those about dancers : they have fewer loves, but even more jealousies, and, on the whole, are very uninteresting personally.

The first female singer at the Paris opera was Mademoiselle de Castilly, who appeared in " Pomone." As she was of noble birth, she obtained from Louis XIV. an edict declaring that " tous les gentilshommes et damoiselles puissent chanter aux dites pièces et représentations de notre Académie royale, sans que pour ce ils soient censés déroger au dit titre de noblesse, ou à leurs priviléges, droits, et immunités."

After her came a series of names which have grown, more or less, into the history of music. The famous Sophie Arnoult was not only a great singer, but also the most brilliant wit of her time; most of the *bons mots* of the eighteenth century were attributed to her. It was she who created the *rôle* of Eurydice in Gluck's " Orphée " on its first performance in 1774.

Mademoiselle Falcon, who appeared in 1832, had an immense success: never had a more magnificent singer been heard; but, after eight years of triumphs, her voice failed suddenly one night in the middle of a performance. It was gone!

The subjects of all the earlier operas represented in Paris were drawn, according to the usage of the period, from mythology, the 'Iliad,' or Greek history. "Jephté," in 1731, was the first piece taken from the Bible. The Archbishop protested against it, and got the representation stopped. But the interdict was soon removed, and from that moment all sources were open to the libretto-maker.

The first *rôle* written for a contralto voice was in Campra's opera of " Tancrède," brought out in 1702. The object was to utilise the superb lower notes of Mademoiselle Maupin.

After these slight indications of scattered points in the records of the Paris Opera, I go on now to such few of my own recollections as have remained clear. The mass of them represent, as I have already said, a kaleidoscopic mist. I see a great confusion of mixed colours and faint sparklings and almost shapeless forms; I am vaguely conscious of much chatter and much laughter; I dimly hear the shouts or the warblings of song, and the crashing or the whispering of music; I hazily perceive lights, diamonds, smiles, shoulders, legs, costumes, trees, mountains, lakes, processions, battles, a variety of crimes, wild loves and equally wild hates, and all the rest that helps to make up a lyric tragedy or a ballet. That, in the main, is what remains to me of long years of Opera; but as nobody else (nobody at least that I have known) can honestly pretend that he preserves much more, and as no other sorts of what is called amusement have left behind them any plainer traces for me, I do not feel justified in addressing any special reproach to the Opera, because my memories of it are so nearly blank. On the contrary, I feel very grateful to it for the little I do remember.

In Gounod's "Tribut de Zamora" (which, I fancy, is not known in England) Madame Krauss filled the *rôle* of a Spanish woman, a native of Zamora, who had been taken prisoner twenty years before by the Moors, her husband being killed fighting and her baby lost, and who had gone mad from the shock. She appears in the piece at forty years of age, after spending half her life amongst her enemies, treated by them with respect precisely because she has lost her reason. At the moment when she comes on, the Spanish girls who are sent each year as tribute, under a disgraceful treaty with the Moors, are brought in from Zamora. One of them is kind to the crazy woman, tries to soothe her, and, sadly, talks to her of Zamora. "Zamora?" repeats the other, wistfully, almost tenderly, as if listening to a far-off echo, "Zamora?" The girl, surprised, asks, "Do you know Zamora?" The dull meaningless answer is again, "Zamora!" Then the girl tells her own story, speaks of her father killed on the ramparts by the Moors, of her mother carried off by them just after she herself was born, of the kind friends who brought her up; and the other listens vacantly, reiterating gently "Zamora!" Suddenly, with a start, the mad woman snatches at the girl, drags her hurriedly to the footlights, stares at her insanely, touches her, pulls her, muttering again and again "Zamora!" struggling, at first feebly; then, by degrees, excitedly; at last, with frantic passion, making terrific efforts to form thought. Her lips part; a hoarse cry comes from them, but it tells nothing; her kindled eyes grow dull again. The girl gazes at her terror-struck; others gather round the maniac and watch her with awe. She falls upon her knees, pulling the girl down to her with the left hand, pointing the other hand out before her into space with an awfulness of idiotic eagerness I have never seen attained by any other actress. Again the moaning cry comes from her, terribly appealing, "Zamora!" With a wild leap she springs to her feet, hurls back her tangled hair, flings up her distorted eyes, and from her lips burst out three hysterical notes, sounding like the opening of a chant. With a strain so fearful that it is positively painful to watch, she crouches down again, glares vacantly before her, and then pours out more notes—this time with half-spoken words! Memory is awaking! Savagely the stress goes on; its fury seems to crush her. Again she falls upon her knees, upon her hands even; she bends down to the ground; lifts herself half up and casts her arms about imploringly, as if supplicating for consciousness. A glimmer shows itself weakly in her eyes; it gains; light is in them; it shines; it flashes; it blazes. Wildly, like a panther from its lair, she springs to her feet again, desperately she throws her ravelled hair behind her, tears off her hood, bares the head that once more begins to hold a mind, and, hesitating, broken, breathless, clutching with her fingers at the air as if to seize support from it, pronounces, in a fearful whisper, "Debout, enfants de l'Ibérie!" And then she goes on muttering "Debout . . . debout!" She stops again, incapable, unknowing. But she has said enough; she has begun the hymn of Zamora! The terrified girl at her side has heard and recognised the words; she seizes gaspingly the mad woman, holds her, calls to her, implores her. The other struggles on. Clearer, plainer, louder, come out the words, "Debout, enfants de l'Ibérie!" Again and again she tries, but she knows not more. At last, after overpowering effort, with all-conquering passion, strained to her fullest height, her head uplifted, her arms stretched out as if to grasp the sky, her eyes a flame of radiance, a flood of bewildered joy, of returned reason, pouring over her, rushing out of her in every gesture, she shouts out, in thundering notes, the whole fierce chant—

"Debout, enfants de l'Ibérie! Haut les glaives et haut les cœurs!
Des païens nous serons vainqueurs, ou nous mourrons pour la patrie!"

Then, turning burningly to the girl, she cries, "And you?" It is her daughter!

It has never been given to me to behold on the stage such a scene as that. Even if I had seen nothing else to recollect, it would have been worth while to go vacantly to the Opera for fifty years in order to wait for that. The first time I was present at it I happened to be in a stage-box, with Madame Krauss ten feet from me. My throat dried, my back grew cold, my heart seemed to stop beating. The effect was almost awful in its intensity. I had always regarded Madame Krauss as a prodigiously powerful dramatic artist, but in that scene she surpassed all I had conceived possible. I need scarcely say that I never talked while that scene was on. The rest of the opera was flat, but those minutes were tremendous; they do indeed stand out in my memories of the Opera.

Another recollection of a very different nature is, for other reasons, almost as fresh in my head. Soon after the present house was opened (I forget the year) Johann Strauss came to Paris with his band, and gave a concert in the staircase of the Opera, which was then still in the glory of its novelty. The concert was for the benefit of the Austro - Hungarian Charity Society of France, and was under the patronage, and indeed under the management, of the Austrian Embassy. All Paris went to it,—ex-kings, ex-princes, and all sorts of other people. The house itself was not opened; the visitors were admitted only to the staircase and its surroundings—that is to say, to the great landings on each floor, to the public *foyer* and *avant-foyer*, and to the colonnades, arcades, and corridors around. This does not seem much in words, but in fact it means an enormous space. And for architectural and ornamental effect nothing more splendid is to be found in Europe; such a grouping of marbles, columns, sculptures, colours, metals, and varied decorations exists nowhere else. The orchestra was placed in the colonnade between the open side of the back of the staircase and the *foyer*. Chairs were against the walls wherever it was possible to put them. The balconies were reserved for the diplomatic body and great personages. The public walked about or sat, and met friends and chatted. A brilliant show it was, and the music was most effective. From the "Blauen Donau" to the "Künstler-Leben," Strauss played almost every one of his compositions, and played them with that quivering swing, that half-dreamy, half-fiery throe, and, above all, with that flickering, caressing hesitation on certain notes, which are all so markedly distinctive of the Vienna manner of performing waltz music. The audience was fairly carried away. The success was enormous. Everybody congratulated Count Kuefstein, the First Secretary of the Austrian Embassy, on having conceived so luminous an idea. A concert in a staircase! But admirable as was the effect, there was a flaw in it. When everybody had arrived (and everybody came early), the staircase itself, which was the centre of everything, as the arena is the centre of a bull - ring, remained absolutely empty. The landings on the first floor were crammed with ball dresses and black coats, but in the middle was a vast hole, white, lustrous, void, engulfing. Not one soul passed up or down or stood upon those blanched marble steps. The chasm grew more and more yawning, cold, and painful, because everybody sat or stood or strolled around it and gazed into it. People seemed to become almost oppressed by it. I, in particular, looked at it with awe, for I was obliged to go away; I had to be elsewhere at eleven. Now going away meant going down that staircase; it meant leaping, like Curtius, into that chasm; it meant the descent of that endless series of white polished slabs (which I had till then admired, but which at that moment I hated) by a man alone in black, with all Paris looking at him. I advanced fearfully to the crest of one of the wide flights and cast my eyes into its depths. It appalled me! I shrank from the awful plunge. It was like forming a storming-party all alone. I wandered away again, and sought in the crowd for some one who looked as if he wanted to go, so that I might follow him. I felt capable of any sort of meanness in order to obtain a leader, or, at all events, a companion. Not one! Everybody stopped stolidly and solidly, and evidently everybody meant to stop until the end. It was already past eleven! At last, with an effort of will and a sentiment of duty, to which I have looked back ever since with admiration, I walked straight to the top step, clenched my teeth (I wanted to shut my eyes too, but I needed them open), and, alone, began the descent. With a determination to appear indifferent, which was never surpassed by the boldest criminal on his way to execu-

tion, I positively sauntered down! Notwithstanding my emotion, I did not hurry. I had
the consciousness that, to the assembled eyes
above, I must have looked like a fly crawling
across a ceiling; but I persisted. In safety
I reached the bottom, disappeared into the
entrance-hall, and breathed. I knew that Paris
loved to scoff, and I expected to be known
thenceforth as "the staircase man"; but, to
my intense relief, I found next day that not a
soul had noticed me, and that all my terror
had been wasted. All the same, I had rather
not do it again.

Another recollection that has remained very
clear to me is of something that happened outside the old house. One night, in January
1858, I had dined in the Champs Elysées, had
lingered there, and had not started for the
Opera till nearly half-past ten. When the cab
that carried me reached the bottom of the
Chaussée d'Antin, it began to go slowly, and
finally pulled up. I found myself in a crowd.
I put my head out and asked the nearest man
what was the matter. He answered excitedly,
"They have tried to assassinate the Emperor;
the Boulevard is barred; you cannot go on."
Then up came a policeman shrieking out the

order to turn back and clear the way. I questioned him, but of course obtained no reply whatever. So I left the cab and went on to the pavement, in the double hope of hearing details and of reaching the Opera on foot.

As everybody was bursting with the news, I was told in half a minute by half-a-dozen eager strangers that an infernal machine had exploded an hour before in the Rue Le Pelletier at the moment when the Emperor and Empress had reached the entrance to the Opera, and that, though neither of them was hurt, their carriage had been half smashed, and numbers of other people had been killed or wounded. I learnt too that every street was closed, that no one was allowed to approach the scene, and that it was idle to dream of getting any farther. The emotion of the mob was immense; horror of the crime and attachment to the Imperial dynasty were loudly professed. I daresay, however, that the suspicion of the presence of detectives listening for evidence stimulated somewhat the rather exaggerated expressions of loyalty I heard around me. In five minutes many descriptions of the explosion had been supplied to me,—most of them in contradiction with each other,—and

I began to feel that I had exhausted the public sources of information available on the Boulevard. So I turned up the Chaussée d'Antin to see if it was possible to get through the Rue de Provence to the Rue Le Pelletier. Before I had gone ten yards I met a friend who told me he had made the attempt, had been turned back by the police, and that he was certain it was idle to try to reach the Opera in any direction whatever. As he hurried on to carry the news to his club, I asked myself suddenly how the people inside the Opera would get away? If nobody on foot could reach the entrance, it was clear that no carriage could arrive there either; and the fate of the ladies began to interest me, especially as the night was cheerless and cold. So I risked saying to a passing policeman, "I have friends in the Opera, and am anxious about them. How will they come out?" For a wonder, he was civil. He answered, "Well, the people, I believe, are coming away now, on foot, round by the back streets. I don't think anybody is allowed to go by the Boulevard. I have seen nothing myself, but that is what I hear from my comrades on the beat." I thanked him, and went on up the Chaussée d'Antin to see if this was true. The crowd was thickening everywhere, for people were arriving from all parts of Paris; feelings of rage and horror, and particularly of shame, were being expressed in loud voices. I pressed on as well as I could, and, with considerable difficulty, squeezed myself at last to the corner of the Rue St Lazare, where the road was closed by a cordon of police. In vain did I appeal to the *sergents de ville*, and urge that I was searching for news of friends; they refused to listen to me or to the dozen other persons who wanted to pass for the same reason. I saw, however, through the shoulders of the people in front of me, that ladies in evening dress were hurrying along the Rue St Lazare, which, at that point, appeared to be kept free for them, and I recognised that a portion of the audience was really escaping that way.

My alarm as to the fate of many acquaintances who, I knew, were at the Opera that night, grew stronger from contact with the emotion of the crowd, and, after a good deal of hesitation, I decided to go to the Rue Tronchet, to inquire if some great friends who lived there, and whose night it was, had returned home. I found the *concierge* asleep, and for half a minute could not make him understand my errand; but when he had woke up and comprehended, he burst into a violent commotion, jumped out of bed, flung on his clothes, and declared that he would go at once to arrest the murderers and pick up the wounded. I had some difficulty in persuading him that he had better leave those functions to the police, and that his duty was to let the servants know what had happened, so that they might make up big fires and have boiling water ready for their mistress and her daughters (who had not come home). So there he and I stopped, wait-ing nervously, listening for steps in the street, till suddenly, at midnight, the bell rang sharply, and in they came, half frozen and terribly up-set. They crouched before the fires and shiv-ered a good deal, from excitement quite as much as from cold. They knew almost less than I did: they had heard the explosion faintly, and did not ask what it meant; but in two or three minutes the news ran like fire round the house; everybody rose; many left their places to inquire; the panic was intense. Suddenly the Emperor and Empress were in their box, came to the front, and, very pale but very self-controlled, faced the audience. Then out burst frantic cheering, wild, furious, unrepressible; it con-tinued for minutes; the women waving handkerchiefs, most of them with tears in their eyes; the sovereigns bowing. It was impossible to think of continuing the performance; the shouting was too tremendous, too enthusiastic, too lasting to leave room for anything else. After a quarter of an hour (to allow time for fetching fresh carriages, instead of the damaged ones) the Emperor and Empress left again, amidst roars and tempests of bravos. Then everybody tried to go away, but found it could not be managed. The street was impassable—partly from damage done, partly from the constant carrying away of wounded (many of whom had been hit in the houses), partly from the stoppage of circulation by the police. So there they all had to remain until a passage was arranged for them, and they could be despatched successively. My friends were too disturbed to remember more, and the little they did know was not at all clear in their heads. They could not find a cab, but were accompanied in their walk by two gentlemen, who, when they had seen them inside their door, hastened to their own homes to relieve the anxiety of their families.

Next morning the details began to take a form; but, if I remember correctly, it was not for two or three days that the authors of the attack were traced and caught.

It was what is known in history as the Orsini plot.

The shake of Madame Bosio has left me an impression of another sort. It was asserted and believed that nobody else ever possessed such a shake, and assuredly it was utterly bewildering. It was smooth as the surface of calm water, rhythmical as the beating of a clock, pulsating as the throb of an engine, enduring as an unknown quantity. No bird ever carolled more trillingly, no star ever scintillated more brilliantly, no diamond ever sparkled more dazzlingly. When we knew that shake was coming, we strained our ears in preparation; while it lasted we held our breath in fascination; when it ended we shouted out applause in intoxication. Of course it was purely mechanical; of course there was no passion in it; of course it was mere vocal dexterity, and in no way the lyrical expression of a feeling; but, all the same, it was as utterly apart in song as was the floating of Taglioni in dance. Amongst the luminosities which here and there light up my memories of the Paris Opera, I put it high.

Another reminiscence is not personal to me, for I was not present at the scenes which compose it; but as it offers interest of a special sort, and as I have often heard the scenes described by those who saw them, I venture to include an allusion to them. Under the influence of Princess Metternich, whose husband had come in the preceding year to France as Austrian Ambassador, "Tannhäuser" was played at the Paris Opera in March 1861. It was hissed, howled at, scorned, and driven off! Paris could not bear it! After three tumultuous representations it was withdrawn. At that time no political feeling was involved: France and Prussia were good friends. The objections were derived not from international enmity, but from profound and thoroughly honest repugnance to the music. The opera-going public of the Second Empire wanted to be amused, not bored,—and "Tannhäuser" bored. A horrid *mot* was made about it: "Ça tanne aux airs et ça embête aux morceaux." The result was that society misbehaved itself. The three evenings were passed in riot—not violent, but contemptuous. It is not often that the public of the Opera rejects the dishes placed before it; on that occasion it did so unmistakably, subject to changing its mind thirty years afterwards. It has now learnt to adore what it then reviled.

I conclude by the end, as is becoming. One of the pleasantest and most amusing of the very various contents of an evening at the Paris Opera, and certainly the portion which affords the most favourable opportunity for observation of local types and manners, is the process of going away. Of course all goings-away are more or less alike, no matter in what country they are performed; but there is, nevertheless, something in the Paris fashion of doing it, something supremely living, which is altogether proper to itself. When the break-up comes; when the staircase is so crowded with descenders from all the floors (rather different from its state that night when I alone was on it) that they have to wait on every step; when, at last, the emerging crowd arrives in the great entrance-hall below, then meetings multiply, and chattering bursts out feverishly, conscious that it has reached its final moments, and that it may be stopped abruptly at any instant by the announcement of the carriage. The groupings and un-groupings of the throng, the shifting shapings of the knots of men and women, are incessant. Goodbye is heard in every tone and language. The scene is made more curious—or at all events more representative — by the mixture of classes. The entire audience is there, from top to bottom. Bonnets and shawls pass side by side with diamonds and resplendent cloaks. And as, at that moment, the doors are no longer guarded, any decent-looking person from outside can come in and contemplate. It is a strange confusion of brilliancy and shabbiness, with a good deal of the always evident effort to look dressed with insufficient means. Typical examples of Paris women are all about. The Duchesse des Sept Croisades, her tongue ejaculating to three men at once; her ugly little petulant face scrambling effervescingly out of a jungle of lace; the infinite elegance of her person spreading radiance around her (sharp contrasts between face and person are special marks of Paris); her rose satin skirts held daintily and rather loftily away from possible obnoxious contacts; her delicate feet reflected glimmeringly on the dark marble of the floor,—is gazed upon by two admiring, though manifestly jealous, work - girls, totally awake and partially attractive, from the gallery.

Three stiff, frumpish Englishwomen, who look excessively out of place in that animated gathering, are staring with wonder at her gestures and her noise, and in half awed whispers are expressing shocked astonishment to each other. In contrast with the Duchesse, Madame de V. stands cold, silent, stately; a very high model of actual Frenchwomen, immensely distinguished, but, like all the rest of them, distinguished rather than aristocratic. The young lady who is known as the " Californian nugget " has removed herself a little apart from the friends who brought her, and is surrounded by a thick circle of young gentlemen, each one of whom is doing his utmost, according to his lights, to persuade her that he alone can make her happy. Regarded as a public exhibition of various devices of love-making (most of them of an extremely elementary nature) the scene may have interest for the worldly philosopher; otherwise it can scarcely be considered to constitute an attractive element of the show. Madame de K. hurries out on the arm of C., leaving behind her, in coruscating waves, the wide wake of glances and admiration, of smiles and salutations, which constitutes *une sortie triomphale.*

Others follow, at each instant, with much *frou-frou* of silk, and with more or less last words, last laughings, and last shruggings. Unfortunately it is invariably the smartest people who get away first, because their servants know their business and bring up the carriages at once; while the dowdies are, as invariably, the last. The perfection of the exhibition endures therefore only for some five minutes: during that period the movement is so fermenting and so vivid, so stirred by the restlessness of its components, so lighted by brilliancies, so diversified by contrasts of types and ways, that it affords a very special view of Paris. There is nothing in it like the beauty of faces one sees in London on similar occasions; but there is an immensely greater air and consciousness of vitality, more indeed, by very far, than in the waiting-hall of any other opera-house in Europe. It is not only vitality, it is almost eagerness; everybody lives acutely for the instant. Suddenly it is finished; all is empty; the gas goes out; another Opera night is over.

CHAPTER XI.

INDOOR LIFE.

NOTWITHSTANDING the amalgamating action of the new international influences which have come into operation during the present century, the ancient differences persist between the exterior habits, the personal looks, and the ways of behaving of the peoples of Europe: they are weakened, but they are not suppressed. The upper classes of various lands — whose educational surroundings are becoming more and more alike — are approximating rapidly to each other in appearance and manners; but even amongst them diversities continue to subsist which, slight as they are in comparison with what they used to be, are, nevertheless, obviously perceptible. And when we look at the masses, variations glare at us. Who has ever crossed a frontier without being impressed by their abundance? In that striking example the suddenness of the change augments its volume; the world of just now has disappeared abruptly, and an utterly transformed one has assumed its place — the dress, the physical aspect, the language, even the movements, of the people round us have become other. After a period of residence in a country, a certain amount of habit forms itself; the eye and ear become accustomed; but at the instant of first entry almost every detail surprises by its strangeness, and evidence enough is supplied to us that, on the outside, nations are still strikingly dissimilar.

I say "on the outside," because what is viewed in ordinary travel is nothing but outside—the railway-station, the port, the street, the shop, the theatre, and the hotel. The indoor life of other lands lies, almost always, beyond the reach of the foreigner: rarely can he enter it at all, or, if he does scrape into it a little, he does not crawl beyond its fringes; he is not admitted to live in it, with it, and of it, and, in most cases, remains uninformed as to its true nature, and as to the realities of national peculiarity which it reveals. Even of a city so much visited and so much talked about as Paris, most travellers know nothing intimately; it is only here and there, by accident, privilege, or relationship, that a few strangers (very few) manage to get inside its doors. The French keep their dwellings resolutely shut; they have small curiosity about foreign persons or things, dislike to have their habits disturbed by intruders; are dominated— especially since 1871—by the bitterest patriotic hates, are in no degree cosmopolitan, are passionately convinced of the superiority of France over the rest of the world,—and, for these reasons, though a very sociable race amongst themselves, shrink instinctively and mistrustfully from people of other blood. Of course there are amongst the great houses of Paris a few in which diplomatists and travellers of rank are habitually received; but those houses constitute exceptions: they stand apart; and even in them it is rare to see foreigners form intimacies with the French. I could mention singular examples of the extreme difficulty of becoming real friends with them, even when circumstances are of a nature to arouse friendship; but such examples would necessitate personal details, and personal details point to names, which, where private individuals are concerned, it is impossible to mention, or even to suggest. Subsidiarily, as regards ourselves in particular, our shyness, and our usually insufficient knowledge of languages, and of current topics of conversation and of the manner of treating them, raise up special barriers in our way. The immense majority of those who go to Paris are, therefore, unable to perceive anything indoors with their own eyes; and it is only from French books and from reports made to them by such fellow-country-men as, in consequence of special circumstances, have been able to look in, that they can learn anything exact of what is going on behind the walls they stare at. As I have looked in long and closely, I venture to add to the second of the two classes of information some of the indoor experiences I have collected.

But, before I begin descriptions, I must make some preliminary observations as regards the situation of the subject.

The strongest of all my notions, in looking back to my experiences in Paris and in comparing them with those I have encountered in other lands, is that, notwithstanding all the superficial contrasts—notwithstanding the differences of material organisation, of ways, and even of habits of thought and of national character—the objects, rules, and practical conditions of existence remain substantially the same everywhere. Exterior looks and details, mannerisms, feelings, temperaments and convictions vary endlessly; but, nevertheless, the main issues come out very nearly identical. It cannot be pretended, for instance, that the French differ fundamentally from the English because they eat a meal called breakfast at half-past eleven, instead of a meal called lunch at half-past one; because they have their children to dine with them, instead of sending them to bed, on bread and milk, at seven; because their servants leave them at a week's notice instead of a month's; because they pay their house-rent on the 15th of January, April, July, and October, instead of what we call quarter-days; because they have (or rather used to have) more elaborate manners than ourselves, and shrug their shoulders more; because they say "two times" for "twice"; or because they talk more volubly than we do. These differences, and a hundred others of the same value, are not in reality differences at all; they are surface accidents—they constitute variety to the eye but not to the mind. However numerous and however evident such outside variations may be, they do not affect the general likeness of all the workings out of human nature any more than the immense diversity of husks affects the methodical germination of the seeds within them. This view may, perhaps, be regarded as incorrect by the ordinary traveller, because to him the smallest newness appears, usually, to be significant, the slightest strangeness full of meaning. But to ancient wanderers, who have had time to grow inured and opportunity to become acclimatised, who have worn off astonishments, who have learnt by long rubbing against others that local demeanours do not change either the head or the heart, the conviction of universal unity becomes unshakable. In their eyes the vast majority of European men and women are animated by exactly the same passions, the same vanities, the same general tendencies, whatever be their birthplace. In their eyes external dissimilarities, which seem at first sight to differentiate nations so markedly, are mere skin-deep tokens, affecting only the secondary and unessential elements of existence, and serving simply as convenient distinctive badges. The contacts of travel have taught them that, though it is natural to attach curiosity to visible national peculiarities, it would be a mistake to expect to find behind them any corresponding divergences of inner essence.

Even national character—which has shown itself everywhere hitherto as a thoroughly enduring reality, and which does not exhibit in any of its developments the faintest signs of coming change—scarcely produces in our day any absolute distinction between the motives and the methods of life-organisation in various countries. It is, of all race-marks, the one which exercises the most effect on public conduct; but I have met nowhere any reasons for believing that it changes the constitution of private and personal existence. By its nature, and for its habitual forms of exhibition, it requires a wider field of operation than it finds indoors. It is strikingly distinct, constant, and energetic in its patriotic and collective manifestations; but its effects are infinitely less evident in small home matters.

Taking nationality as an accumulative designation for the entire group of diversities which distinguish nations from each other, it cannot be said to govern, in any appreciable degree, the essential composition of the indoor life of peoples. It works strongly in other directions, but scarcely at all in that one. It does not ıntroduce, in any land, home elements which are entirely unknown elsewhere.

For this reason, in speaking of the indoor life of Paris, I shall not have much to say of radical differences; there are scarcely any. Even details, with all their copious variety, do not preserve, on examination, the vividness of contrast which they present at first sight. Just as moral principles (under similar conditions of education) exist everywhere in broad averages; just as they show themselves, all about, in fairly equal proportions—like vice and virtue, intelligence and stupidity, health and disease—so do the main conditions of indoor life run, in all countries, in parallel grooves, slightly twisted, here and there, by superficialities. What there is to tell, therefore, is about impressions rather than about facts, about sensations rather than about sights, almost indeed about resemblances rather than about differences.

But, what is indoor life? To some it represents little more than mere family existence; to others, on the contrary, it is but an additional name for society; to others, again, it represents a temporary separation from the world, during which we put off the constraints in which we enwrap ourselves in public, and relapse momentarily into the undistorted realities of self. With these wide oppositions of interpretation (and there are more besides), it is impossible for any of us to speak of indoor life with the certainty that we mean by it the same thing as others do. And not only does it change its aspects, its objects, and its significations with the individual point of view of each of us, but also with the persons at whom we happen to look. I speak, therefore, of the indoor life of Paris for myself alone, describing not so much what I have seen in it as what I have felt in it; recognising heartily that every other witness has a right to disagree with me, and recognising it all the more because, on such a subject, it is on instincts and ideas proper to each one, rather than on indisputable verities evident to all, that spectators base their very varying judgments.

On one doctrine only is everybody likely to be in accord with everybody else. That doctrine is that indoor life, whatever else it may be taken to import, implies essentially the life of women, and that its nature shifts about with the action of the women who create it. This doctrine, true everywhere, is especially true of Paris; for there, more than anywhere, certain women stand out before and above all their fellows as the national producers of the brightest forms of its indoor life. That life is made by them and for them; they manufacture it in its perfected attractiveness; and, above all, they typify it. They are so thoroughly both the composers and the actors of the piece, that a description of it does not signify much more than a description of the women who play it.

But this is true of very few indeed amongst the women of Paris. They all lead, in general terms, the same sort of indoor life, so far as its outlines are concerned; yet scarcely any of them help to shape or guide it in what constitutes its national aspects. Acquaintance with it shows that the mass of them follow it passively, but neither originate it nor enkindle it. They are content with dull humdrum existences, and take no part in the active composition of the typical aspects of the place. They do their duty placidly, as wives, mothers, and housekeepers; they are, most of them, worthy, excellent, estimable persons; most of them smoulder in inertness. I remember how astonished I was at the beginning, when I was still under the influence of the fanciful teach-

ings of my youth, to discover, by degrees, that
Paris women were not, as I had been assured
by my British instructors of those days, all
worldly, all pleasure-seeking, all love-making,
all dress-adoring; but that the majority of them
were quiet, steady, home-cherishing, devoid of
all aggressive personality, animated by a keen
sense of moral duty. Such is their nature
still, modified only, in certain cases, by the
action of that wonderful French faculty, adaptability, which fits those who possess it for
any social or even leading *rôle*. Unluckily, the
faculty itself is rare, and, of those who own
it, a good many have neither the ambition nor
the power to use it, and remain, just as most
women do in other lands, unproductive in their
nullity. They are French in the details of
their ways and habits; but the great heap of
them might just as well be anything else, so
far as any national fruitfulness is concerned.
It is not they who stand out as the makers
and the beacons of the bright life of Paris;
that part is played by a very restricted minority, which, small as it is, lights up so vividly
the circles round it, that it seems to represent
the nation all alone before the world. The
fireside goodnesses of the majority are to be

seen, almost in the same forms, in any other country; but the fertile arts and the sparkling devices of the minority are special to Paris: they cannot be found outside it ; and, even there, they are utterly exceptional. But, scarce though they be, they constitute, all by themselves, the most striking elements of indoor life, for they alone bring into evidence the processes employed by the higher Paris woman.

By the " higher Paris woman " I do not mean the woman of the higher classes only, but the woman of the higher capacities, whatever be her class, provided only she applies them. It is essential to insist on this, for in Paris capacity does not necessarily follow class. It is, of course, more frequent amongst the well-born, because of their advantages of heredity, of training, and of models: but birth alone cannot bestow it; it is to be found in every educated layer ; like adaptability, it may be discovered anywhere. Capacity, in the sense I have in view, may be defined, roughly and approximately, as the power of creating a home to which everybody is tempted to come, and of reigning in that home over all who visit it. It is a purely social ability, for it can only be exercised in society ; but it is attainable by any woman who has the consciousness of its germ within her, and who has, or can manufacture, the tools and the opportunities to develop it. The European reputation of the social life of Paris proceeds almost exclusively from the fitness of a few women in each group. The men count for very little —the other women for nothing at all. The other women make up the universal crowd, with its universal qualities and its universal defects: they manage conscientiously their own little lives, but they exhibit nothing of true French brilliancies, and it is those brilliancies alone which attract the attention and excite the admiration of the world.

But, alas! the woman who does possess the brilliancies is disappearing rapidly; she is becoming almost a creature of the past; which fact supplies another motive for trying to describe her while some patterns of her still exist.

And now, having explained the situation in its main lines, I can begin to try to sketch such elements of the indoor life of Paris as seem to me to be worth remembering.

It follows from what I have already said that that life is divided into two clearly distinguishable divisions—the work of the mass, and the work of the minority. In speaking of the characteristics of the mass, it is difficult to use general statements, because no wording, however elastic, can apply to everybody; because there are exceptions to every rule; because the little diversities of natures and of ways (even when all are dominated by the same principles of action) are endless. All that can be done safely is to indicate certain main features of temperament and behaviour, and to declare expressly that those features are not universal, and that no single picture can portray every face.

The ordinary Paris woman, who makes up the mass, is rarely interesting as a national product. There is seldom anything about her that is markedly different from the woman of elsewhere. Occasionally she dresses well; occasionally she wears her clothes well, and, in that matter, does stand, here and there, somewhat apart; occasionally she is smart, but much more often she is not smart at all, and is sometimes altogether dowdy. When it was the fashion to be *comme il faut*, nearly every woman did her best to reach the standard of the period, because it corresponded to her innate idea of quiet. But now that strong effects have taken the place of distinction, she has, in many cases, become indifferent and neglects herself. Superiorities of any sort are rare in her, just as they are elsewhere. Of course she has local peculiarities, but peculiarities do not necessarily constitute superiorities. In one respect, however, the French woman throughout the land does stand high,—she possesses, as a rule, vigorous home affections: they are, indeed, so vigorous that, taking her class as a whole, I doubt whether the corresponding women of any other race arrive at the deep home tenderness which she shows and feels. Her respect for the ties and duties of relationship is carried so far that, under its impulsion, there are positively (although she is not always quite pleased about it) examples of three generations living permanently together, apparently in harmony! Her attitude towards her children is one of great love: they live, in most cases, entirely with her, and constitute the main object of her existence. I do not pretend that the bringing up which results therefrom is the best in the world — that question lies outside the present matter—but I do maintain that a very striking feature of the indoor life of Paris, regarded in its family aspects, is the intensity of the attachment and devotedness of the women to their parents and their children, and their sympathy for other relations. Their husbands, perhaps, are not invariably included in this overflowing sweetness. Of course there are women who care nothing for either their children or any one else; but the rule is, incontestably, throughout all ranks, that all are strangely full of the home tie.

The perception of family duties is, indeed, so keen, as a general state, that the whole race obtains from it a basis for the construction of home happiness in a solid (though stolid and prosy) shape, and, if happiness could be built up with one material alone, could reasonably hope to enjoy a good deal of it. Unfortunately, however, for everybody else as well as for the French, such little happiness as seems to exist about the earth is derived evidently from the joint action of so many and such composite causes (and from individual character even more than from any outer cause whatever), that one single faculty, no matter how important or how robust it may be, does not suffice to beget it. In the particular case of the average Paris woman, we cannot help recognising, whenever we get a clear sight of her indoors, with her mask off, in a condition of momentarily ungilded authenticity, that, notwithstanding the acuteness of her family sentiment, she obtains from it no more active happiness than falls to the lot of her less family-loving neighbour in other lands.

If she extracts distinct contentment from any one source, it is from a totally different one — from the consciousness that, with all the habitual dulness of her existence (I speak, of course, of the average mass), she possesses, in certain cases, a handiness proper to herself, a quick perceptivity, a faculty of absorption, appropriation, and reproduction of other people's ideas, a capacity for utilising occasions. In this direction she does possess sometimes a national superiority. But this most useful characteristic is very far from universal: the great majority of Paris women do not possess an atom of it; and furthermore, when it does exist, it is, in most of its examples, rather mental than practical, — it shows itself in words rather than in acts. For instance, the women of the present day are rarely good musicians; scarcely any of them can paint, or sing, or write; very few indeed can cook or make dresses; very few read much, in comparison with the English or the Germans; but a portion of them can talk sparklingly of what they pick up from others. Of this form of talent (when she has it) the Paris woman is, with reason, proud; and satisfied vanity is to many natures — to hers in particular — a fertile root of joy. Speaking generally, and excluding all the heavy people, mental handiness may be said to be one of her distinguishing marks. She is enthusiastic about moral qualities, especially when she thinks she can attribute them to herself; but, as a rule, she puts above them in her desires the capacities of personal action which can aid her to get on. Her nature is not often either generous or liberal, but it is occasionally very religious. She has a tendency to attach importance to small things; the sense of proportion and of relative values is often weak in her, — with the consequence that she follows, half instinctively, a life in which trifles play a large part, and such powers of productive usefulness as she may possess are a good deal wasted on unessential occupations.

Amongst the trading classes, where the wives so often share the business work of the husbands, there is sometimes a look of real solidity of purpose; but it cannot be said that in the middle and upper ranks, notwithstanding the abundance of their general virtues, there is much appearance of steady earnestness. There is eagerness rather than energy, vivacity rather than vigour, restlessness rather than industry. I should not like to say that the ordinary Paris woman possesses no earnestness, but I have often asked myself whether, as a rule, she really has any. The fact that their language contains no word for earnestness, or indeed for any of the forms of thoroughness, does seem to suggest that the French have no need of expressing the idea which the word conveys; though when they are told this they answer triumphantly, "But we have *sérieux!*" Now *sérieux*, which is employed both as a substantive and an adjective, does not in any way correspond to earnestness or earnest; it implies a certain gravity, a certain ponderosity, and even, in many cases, a certain portentous solemnity. The state is common to the two sexes, and to be thought *sérieux* is an object of ambition to some men and to some women. It does not involve knowledge, or labour, or determination ; but it does purport supremacy over the follies of life. Of course there are " *des personnes sérieuses,*" who are so by natural inclination, and whose *sérieux* means merely quietness, correctness, and preference for calm duty; in all of which, again, there is nothing of what we understand by earnestness. The absence of earnestness is not compensated by the presence of *sérieux* (when it is present), and there remains, on the whole, a worthy, affectionate, dutiful life, often a little gloomy, sometimes intelligent, scarcely ever intellectual,—life like what it is anywhere else, neither more brilliant nor more productive, but with differences of detail.

The women who lead this average life have, naturally, their social occupations too, their social vanities, and their struggles after place; some of them possess distinct aptitudes for the little battle, and fight it with what they conceive to be success. But that side of the subject is only really interesting amongst the minority, to whom I am coming in an instant.

The men generally (unless they have fixed occupations) live the indoor life of their families,

excepting during the time they pass. in the
little room which most of them possess under
the title of "*le cabinet de Monsieur.*" What
they do in that little room I have never discovered to my satisfaction, though I have employed almost half a century in searching.
They seem contented, but they do not aid
much to shape the family existence—that is
the function of their wives. It is surprising
that men who exhibit so much movement,
and even so much excitement, about outdoor
things, should be so passive and inoperative
indoors. There is nothing to be said about
them in connection with the subject I am
discussing.

The material conditions of the life of the
mass are, on the whole, comfortable. On
many points there are sharp differences
between French arrangements and ours: there
is generally, for instance, far more finish of
furniture with them, and somewhat more
finish of service with us. The look of the
rooms is certainly prettier and gayer in Paris
than in London,—partly because the walls,
the chairs, the tables, are more decorative,
and the colours of the stuffs and hangings
lighter and brighter; partly because chintz

coverings are never seen, the clearness of the air allowing everything to remain unhidden. There are many more mirrors; ornaments lie about more abundantly, and in greater variety of nature and effect. The grouping of the whole is far less regular, less stiff, more intimate. This advantage is most marked in the drawing-rooms; it continues, in a less degree, in the bedrooms; there are traces of it in some of the dining-rooms. But the setting out of the table is almost always inferior to ours, both in detail and as a picture; and (barring the great houses) the servants wait with less attention and less experience. I speak, of course, in the most general terms and of the broad average, taking no notice of the exceptions, on either side. As regards comfort, it can scarcely be asserted that the inhabitants of either of the two countries live better, on the whole, than the others.

Most Paris women stay so much indoors that their material surroundings at home are of particular importance to them. Many of them go out only once a-day, for an hour or two perhaps. The vast majority have still, notwithstanding the change that is coming over them, no outdoor amusements. Indeed, viewing amusement as a serious occupation, there is vastly more of it in London than in Paris, or in any other city in the world. No people run after amusement so insatiably as the English : they are at it all day, in some form. The Parisians, on the contrary, take their pleasures mainly in the evening, and almost always rest in peace till the afternoon; those who ride or do anything in the morning are infinitely few. As a practice, they do not dress for dinner when they are alone; the mass of them give scarcely any dinner-parties to friends or acquaintances; they leave them to the minority, who employ them largely; but, as a consequence of their family attachments, they constantly have relatives to share their *gigot*. There are no day-nurseries for children, who live in the drawing-room, or a bedroom, with their mothers, and learn there to become little men and women. There are no old maids, mainly because almost every girl marries young : if any fail to find a husband (which happens rarely), they vanish out of sight; unmarried women over thirty are scarcely known or heard of in Paris; the thousand duties to which they apply themselves in England are left undischarged in France. Finally, no visitors come to stay in a Paris house—partly because it is not the custom, partly because there is no spare room, which is the better reason of the two.

I come now to the minority, to the higher women, to something in the indoor life of the place which is unlike what is found elsewhere. The higher women differ in nearly every detail of their attitude from the mass which I have just described—almost as much, indeed, as art differs from nature. Excepting that they too are, usually, good mothers, there is scarcely anything in common between them and the others. Just as the mass live for the home, so do the minority live for the world; and, for a student of the world and its ways, there is not to be discovered a more perfect type, for it is a product of the very highest worldly art, worked up with skill, will, and finish. It is all the more a product of pure art because, as I have already remarked, the higher Paris woman may be found outside the highest social class, and may be manufactured out of any suitable material. The particular position which is created by birth is not indispensable to her: it bestows a brilliancy the more, but that is all. The woman of whom I am speaking may be of any rank, provided she possesses the requisite abilities, and provided she can gather round her a group worthy of her handling. And this is the more true because, with some evident exceptions, social station in Paris does not depend exclusively, or even mainly, on the causes which bestow it elsewhere,—on birth or name, on title or on money : they all aid, they aid largely; but not one of them is absolutely requisite. Even money, powerful as it is, is less conquering in Paris than in London, as certain persons have discovered, who, after failing to get recognised to their satisfaction in the former city, have succeeded in thrusting themselves to the front in the latter. The Paris woman who wins position, even if she possesses these four assistants, owes her victory, not to them, but to herself, to her own use of the powers within her. She merits minute description, both in her person and her acts. But here a difficulty arises. Her acts can be set forth in as much detail as is needed; but her person — and, for the results that she begets, her person is as important as her acts — cannot be depicted in English.

The reason is, that the ideas which dominate us as to the uses to which our language ought to be applied prevent us from handling it freely on such a subject. There are limits to the application of English, limits which we have laid down for ourselves, limits which exclude the possibility of treating glowingly certain topics without appearing to be ridiculous. To speak of the feminine delicacies of a thorough Paris woman, to show their influence on the crowd around her and on the life she leads, and to dissect their sources, their manifestations, and their consequences, as the French do, would be regarded by the British public as unworthy of the solidity of British character. So, as her person cannot be faithfully outlined without French appreciations of its elegancies, without employing French methods of photographic portraiture, and without painting in French colours the admiration it inspires; and as those French appreciations, methods, and colourings would be regarded as "gushing" in English, the person of the Paris woman must remain undrawn by English pens. The difficulty does not proceed from the English writer, but from the English reader: the English language is as capable as French is of telling the tale of winning feminine refinements; but our feeling is against the employment of it for such frivolous purposes. We do not produce the same human works of art, and are not accustomed to English descriptions of them. The French pages which narrate the perfections of women, which write of details in detail and of graces with grace, are read in France with eager interest, because of the inherent attraction of the subject to the French mind, and of the amazing dexterity and finish which, from long practice, have been acquired in the handling. The story is so vivid that we see and hear reality, so seductive that we bow before charm, so adroitly told that we marvel at the author's cunning. Even the English (a good many of them at all events) read all this in French with keen appreciation; but in their present mood they would call it silly in English. Our literature loses by this exclusion — which extends to other topics besides Frenchwomen—a quantity of opportunities which many writers would, it may be presumed, be delighted to utilise, but dare not, for fear of being scoffed at. It is altogether inexact to argue that "the genius of the French language"—a much employed but nearly meaningless expression—lends itself to wordings which cannot be rendered in other tongues; it is not genius but habit which explains those wordings. French has no monopoly of the phrases needed to delineate personal elegance; neither has the French mind any exclusive property of the sentiment of physical symmetries, or of the faculty of analysis of delicate perceptions and of the sensations aroused by those perceptions. Both the thinkings and the wordings would be forthcoming elsewhere, if only readers wanted them. The Belgians, for instance, who use French, have no more of them than we have, for the reason that, like us, they do not feel the need of them. As things stand at present, the person of the higher Parisienne cannot be depicted diagnostically in English: that element of the subject must be left out here, which is a pity, not only because it is the prettiest part of it, but also because the exclusion lessens the field of discussion of Paris indoor life. Her work alone remains to be talked about.

The higher Frenchwoman, in the time of her full glory, was essentially a leader of men: from the Fronde downwards, the history of France was full (fuller far than that of any other land) of evidence of the influence of women on its progress; but that influence, after waning steadily since the Revolution, went entirely out of sight with the solidification of the actual republic. After the war of 1870 it struggled on, under increasing difficulties, until MacMahon resigned; since his time it has disappeared altogether. The banishment of the men of the well - born classes from all share in the government of the country (not only because they are Conservatives, but even more because others want the places which, for the greater part, they formerly occupied) has necessarily brought about the repudiation of the women too; and such of them as are not well - born suffer in sympathy, for their cause is common. The republicans avow that "*la république manque de femmes,*" but it will never win the higher women to it until, amongst other things, it makes a place for them to work. At present they are entirely shut away from contact with the public life of France; they have lost all empire over the events of the time, and, in consequence, they themselves have weakened. It would be inexact to call them politicians, in the English sense of the word; but they are animated by a need of personal performance and productivity which cannot be satisfied without dabbling, from however far off, in current affairs. Their intelligence has always sought for spheres of action; but Liberty, Equality, Fraternity—"*un songe entre deux mensonges*" — have now suppressed all spheres of action for them outside the walls of their drawing-rooms. The so-called governing classes, to which, directly or indirectly, a good many of them belonged, are replaced by the *nouvelles couches;* the overthrow of the classes as national instruments has entailed the overthrow of the women as a national force, and has reduced them to a purely social function, which gives insufficient play to their aspirations, and thrusts them back into themselves. The rupture between society and the republic is complete, and, apparently, unmendable. Both lose by it; but society loses the most, because, though the republic can prosper ruggedly without society, the women of society (whatever be their birth) cannot breathe healthily without the position and the occupation which they formerly obtained from contact with authority.

This decline affects them individually as well as collectively, and because of it (amongst other causes) they no longer present the very marked

national lineaments which once belonged to
them. There is still something to tell, both
of their cleverness and of their attractiveness;
but, while the proportion of attractiveness
remains considerable, the proportion of cleverness has largely diminished. As it was, in
great part, by cleverness actively employed
—effective, operative, prolific cleverness—that
the foremost Paris women won the bright
place they once held before Europe, it is evident that the lessening of that cleverness
renders them less instructive to study. And
they themselves, some of them at least, are
at this moment, in other directions, wilfully
damaging their attractiveness too, by leaping
into the wave of masculinity which the English
have set surging, and by allowing their infinite
femininity of other days to be drowned by it.
Many of them have taken up and, with the
ardour of neophytes, have already surpassed
us in, the most conspicuous of the new exercises which, under pretext of physical development, English women have invented.
If size is to become the chief ambition of
women, if the merits of girls and wives are
to be measured by length, we ought to ask
the Germans and the Swedes how they man-

age to produce giants. They have plenty of women six feet high, feminine and gentle in their way, who could not distinguish between a golf-club and a billiard-cue, or between a racquet and a battledore, and who, though they may have had in their childhood some moderate practice of gymnastics, have never given an hour to rude games, to riding on a bicycle, or to any of the recent forms of romping. It is possible that, some day, women will once more become desirous to remain women; but, for the moment, the example offered by the English is unfeminising France, and that effect, in addition to political enfeeblement, renders many of the Paris women of to-day different indeed from what they used to be. Yet, in some of their examples, they retain a portion of their former selves, and continue to be something else than others are. They are changed, lamentably changed, as a general type; but memorials of their former merit are still discoverable.

Manner, movement, dress, and talk are the weapons of the higher Paris woman who continues to be exclusively a woman. She employs them all in her relations with the world, on her day, at her dinners, at her parties. On her day a mob may come to her, because her door is open to her entire acquaintance; but, unless she is a personage, her dinners and her parties are usually kept small. A view of her on her day is interesting, perhaps the most interesting feminine spectacle in Paris, for she shows more of her varied skill on that occasion than on any other. She has to be everything to everybody at once; to graduate her welcomes; to measure her smiles; to give their full rights of greeting and of place to all her visitors, but no more than the right of each; and, above all, notwithstanding this calculated adjustment, to send everybody away with the conviction that they, in particular, were the very persons she most wished to see. The power of listening is, in such a case, almost more important than the power of speaking, for there is no flattery so irresistible as to lead stupid people to believe you are intensely interested in what they say. Towards those whom she wishes to impress, she exhibits herself in her utmost winningness, according to what she imagines to be their accessible sides. To this one she throws scintillant talk; she dazzles that one with the elegancies of her person; to another she is all deep sympathy and tender feeling; of a fourth she inquires gravely, as if such subjects were the one study of her hours, whether the experiments in the liquefaction of carbon are progressing hopefully, or who will be the next successful candidate at the *Académie*. There is certainly great labour in the process: the tension of the mind is augmented by the longing for success, and by unceasing attention to physical effect as an essential aid to that success. But, to a thorough woman of the world, conceive the delights of success! What must she feel when her last visitor has left,—when she looks back over the four hours she has just passed, and tells herself that every one has been conquered by her, and has carried away a deep impression of her charm? The scene can be beheld in Paris only, — at least I have not discerned it in the same perfection in any other society: it is far away the most special picture of its indoor life; it shows the typical Frenchwoman in her most finished development, which no one else can attain. But how rare it is!

At dinner her doings are equally complete, but not the same. She is differently dressed. She is "*en peau*" (I mention, for those who may not be aware of it, that this is the modern expression for *décolletée*); and with the change of covering comes change of bearing, for the perfect Paris woman has a bearing for every gown. Just as the nature of the dress itself indicates its purpose, its meaning, and the hour at which it is to be worn, so does she herself associate her ways with that meaning. The movements of her bare shoulders and bare arms at dinner are not identical with the movements of the morning or the afternoon in a high *corsage* and long sleeves. They have another story to relate, another effect to produce, other duties to discharge; her measurement of their value and their functions is quite different. The action of the hands, again, is in full view; their language can be spoken out; their eloquence can exercise its completest force; she talks with them as with her tongue. In pleased consciousness of her delightfulness she sits in the centre of her table, casts her glances and her words around her, undulates with varied gesture, and is again, in thorough meaning and result, the typical Parisienne.

And yet, by one of the contradictions with which the entire subject is piled up, she is unable to bestow immortality on the memory of her dinners. That memory disappears, for, incomprehensible though it be, there is nothing which mankind in its thanklessness forgets like dinners: there is nothing which in gratitude we ought to remember more; there is nothing which in reality we remember less. This fact of the utter fading away of dinners is a puzzle to all people who have passed their lives in dining, with full recognition of the superlative importance of the process. Scarcely any of them recollect anything precise about the thousand banquets at which they have filled a place. They agree, generally, that they have entirely forgotten what they have eaten, that they have almost forgotten what they have seen, that they have the feeblest consciousness of the people they have met, and that their only relatively clear remembrance is of the bright talk they have heard occasionally at table. The ear is the only organ which retains really lasting impressions; the tongue preserves nothing, and the eye scarcely anything. I believe that, with the exception of a few professional *gourmets* (a class that is becoming everywhere more and more rare), this is the condition of mind of nearly everybody who is in a position to form an opinion on the subject. One of my acquaintances, who dined diversifiedly about Europe, became so convinced in early life that dinners

are inevitably forgotten, that he preserved from
his outset the *menus* and lists of guests, with
the placing at table, of all the repasts at which
he assisted. When I saw his collection it had
grown into several folio volumes. The entries
in it were made with such precision, that, dis-
covering in it one of my own cards with a date
on it, and asking what it signified, I was told
by my acquaintance that its object was to regis-
ter the fact that he had dined with me alone
on the day indicated. He, at all events, had
succeeded in preventing himself from falling into
the universal oblivion: he considered, probably
with truth, that he was the only man in European society who was animated by the real
reconnaissance de l'estomac, and who could reconstitute, with becoming thankfulness and certainty, the details of every dinner he had eaten.
At the actual moment of dinner we feel, of
course, a more or less keen perception of the
merits or demerits of the feast. But the perception does not endure: even bad and gloomy
dinners are forgotten, just as thoroughly as
good and gay ones. The explanation is, it
seems to me, that we dine too often; one dinner drives out the effect of another. If we had
only one dinner in our lives, how we should

remember it!   Of the four great elements of dinners—food, people, spectacle, and talk—the talk alone, as I have already observed, dwells on, in some degree, in our thoughts.   No one can fail to recognise that cookery is valueless as a permanent cause of memory of dinners: it has but a merely momentary effect; it does not merit the front place it is too commonly supposed to occupy in the general constitution of a repast; it stands, on the contrary, last in durability amongst the four constituents. Scarcely any of the older students of dining persist in giving serious thought to food, partly because of weakening digestions, mainly because they have learnt from long practice that the real pleasure of a dinner is derived from another source.   They see in it not an occasion for eating, but a most ingenious and soul-contenting arrangement for bringing men and women intimately together under conditions which supply many stimulants and brightnesses—an arrangement which enables them to show themselves at their best, and which terminates the day with lustre, like a luminous sunset.

Now, talk at dinner—the one enduring element of the ceremony—can never reach its full radiance without women: and here comes

in the application of these considerations to
the Parisienne, for it is her talk which raises
dinner to the high place it occupies in Paris.
A womanless dinner may not be quite so dismal as a night without stars, or a desert without water; but it may fairly be compared to a
tree without leaves, to a sea without ships, or
to a meadow without buttercups. Somewhere
in the sixties I dined with M. Emile de Girar-
din (I name him because he was a public man),
in that admirable house in the Rue Pauquet
which he called his "thatched hut." He was
famous for his dinners, and on the occasion
to which I refer the cookery was supreme—
so supreme indeed that I told myself at the
time I had never partaken of such a dinner:
that shapeless fact is still in my memory; but
what there was to eat, or who was there, I
have utterly forgotten. I know only it was a
dinner of men — that is to say, not a dinner
at all in the great social meaning of the term.
Women and talk alone make dinner, especially
in Paris, where the value of the women and
the talk reaches its highest possibilities. If
we forget all about it as soon as it is over,
that is not the fault of the Parisiennes; they,
at all events, have done their utmost to induce

us to remember. Certain Paris dinners provide, probably, a more complete supply of
social satisfaction than can be extracted from
any other single source. They give us what
we want at the moment in its best conceiv-
able form, with all the components and surroundings that can furnish outside assistance.
Of course dinners are more or less alike everywhere; of course the foundations and the
general nature of the structure reared upon
them cannot vary widely; but in the double
sensation of serenity and complacency on the
one hand, and of inspiring allurement on the
other, Paris possesses in a few houses an
atmosphere which cannot be breathed anywhere else, and which constitutes a true international distinction.

It is possible that, to the inexperienced eye,
the charm of this would not be as evident as
it becomes on intimate knowledge of it. We
like best what we are most accustomed to;
strange ways rarely please us at first — the
habit of them needs to be formed before we
can appreciate them. There is an involuntary
shrinking from the new and the unknown; it
is only after time and usage that, in most
cases, we become fit to comprehend the merit

of practices that we were not brought up to admire. But when habit has had opportunity to grow, when experience has enabled us to base our judgments on long comparison, then, at last, we recognise excellences which do not strike new - comers. I insist particularly on this consideration, because it explains not only the source of the opinions I hold, but also one of the reasons why others may differ from those opinions.

A Paris evening-party is nearly the same process as a "day"—in other clothes, and with more facility for walking about. There is nothing to be said of it that I have not said already. I will, however, mention one recollection that has a relation to its aspects. The first time I was present at a ball in Paris, I was struck by the singular freshness of the colours of the dresses, after the tints I had known in England: it was not the making of the dresses that I noticed, but their shades, which had a bloom that astonished me. I soon lost, from constant view, the power of comparing; but at first, before my eyes had become trained, it seemed to me that even the whites were whiter, brighter, more intense than any I had seen before, while all the other hues looked

more transparent and more living. I make
no attempt to explain the impression I received, but of its reality I am certain.
Whether the distinction still endures I cannot say (new arrivers alone could now judge
of that); but at the moment, while the sense
of it lasted, it served to mark a visible difference between the balls of Paris and of London. In all else, save some few unimportant
contrasts of manners and of details, evening-
parties have seemed to me about the same
everywhere, and I can think of nothing about
them that is really proper to Paris. The
women exercise at them an attraction on the
people round which is more general and less
individual than at dinners: there is space;
the spectators are far more numerous; the
women are more completely seen; but, all the
same, they dominate less. I have always
fancied that, for this reason, the true Paris
woman is somewhat wasted at an evening-
party; she is too much in the crowd; she
may be admired, but she does not always
rule. Her one advantage at night receptions
is that she can stand and walk about, and
can produce effects of motion which are
denied to her at dinner.

This sort of life in Paris is not, after all, more worldly than the same existence is elsewhere. Wherever amusement is lifted to the position of the first object of existence, the moral effect on those who pursue it is virtually the same: there may be shades of local difference, but the tendency of the mind grows everywhere alike. It would therefore be unfair to attribute any special frivolity to Paris because small sections of its society achieve extreme brilliancy of worldliness; just as it would be unfair to praise it specially because other classes are particularly worthy of esteem. In the universal average of good and bad, Paris stands on the same general level as other capitals; but in glistening pleasantness it rises, here and there, above them all. The reason is that the higher Paris women possess usually both intelligence and elegance, the two qualities which society specially requires, which are rarely found together elsewhere (at all events in the same proportions and with the same effects), and the union of which has won for the best examples of Parisiennes the world-wide reputation they have enjoyed. Their superiority still exists, but how long it will continue to endure remains to be

seen : it is weakening fast from the progres-
sive disappearance of the women who, thus
far, have maintained it. If it does vanish
altogether, Paris will become like any other
place, with the same respectabilities and the
same dulnesses ; but its indoor life will have
left behind it a history and a memory proper
to itself, and some day, perhaps, its women will
wake up again and will reassume the feminine
graces, the feminine capacities, and, above all,
the true feminine intelligence which were so
delightfully distinctive of their mothers.

That they may recover fully those graces,
those capacities, and that intelligence, is one
of the earnest wishes I offer to a race amongst
which I no longer live, but to which I owe
many of the happinesses and most of the
brightnesses of my life, and towards which,
until my thoughts cease, I shall feel deep and
solidly founded gratitude.

THE END.